THE

OF HISARTA

THE HERMIT
OF HISARYA

Hannah Howe

Goylake Publishing

Goylake Publishing, Iscoed, 16A Meadow Street, North Cornelly, Bridgend, Glamorgan. CF33 4LL

ISBN: 978-0-9932458-9-3

Printed and bound in Britain by Imprint Digital, Exeter, EX5 5HY

The Sam Smith Mystery Series by Hannah Howe,
available in print, as eBooks and audio books

To my family,
also to Dragan Danev, Ivanka Daneva
and all my Bulgarian friends, with love

Chapter One

My fiancé, Dr Alan Storey, was a leading psychologist and, as a distinguished member of his profession, he'd been invited to Plovdiv, Bulgaria, to speak at an international conference on psychology. On receiving the invitation, Alan had suggested that yours truly, Samantha Smith, a humble enquiry agent, should tag along to enjoy a holiday in the sunshine. So, and for the first time, I found myself sitting in an aeroplane, gazing at my fellow passengers, wondering about our holiday, worrying about the flight and the neglect I was inflicting on my agency.

As I stretched my legs, I considered that aeroplanes are the TARDIS in reverse – they seem huge on the outside, yet are small and cramped on the inside; and I speak as a petite five foot five. Still, the seats in the Airbus were comfortable and with Alan at my side, I could relax. Maybe.

Sensing my anxiety, Alan turned to me and smiled. He placed a hand over my hand and gave my fingers a gentle squeeze. "Have you been to Bulgaria before?" he asked, his tone light, relaxed, at ease.

"I've never flown before," I confessed.

"But you've been abroad before?"

"Yeah, to France, on a school trip. We travelled to Brittany, by ferry. The sea was like a millpond on our way over, yet I still managed to be sick. On the way back, the channel was choppy and I threw up for five hours, non-stop. Needless to say, that was the beginning and end of my educational holidays."

"Well," Alan sighed, "we'll soon be up in the air and before you know it, we'll be in Plovdiv."

I nodded, wishing that I could share his confidence and sense of ease.

We were sitting side by side, in two seats to the left of the aisle, Alan nearest the window. He gazed through the window, to no one, to nothing in particular, his handsome features calm and serene, his hand still resting on mine, his fingers, absentmindedly, circling my engagement ring.

"My agency's been running for six years," I reflected, "and this is my first proper holiday in that time."

"Then you're overdue a break."

"I know. But what about my clients...?"

"You have nothing to worry about. After all, Faye's in charge. She'll take care of things; Faye's a capable woman; what could go wrong?"

My friend and flatmate, Faye Collister, had volunteered to mind the store. Faye was kind and conscientious, though a little flaky at times with her obsession for neatness and order. She would take care of Marlowe, my office cat, and tend to business until my return. I liked and trusted Faye, yet it was *my* agency so I did feel a pang of guilt and a hint of regret at abandoning my clients and their woes.

A glance through the window told me that an aeroplane was circling overhead, waiting to land, that the sky was blue and clear, that the sun was shining on a perfect summer's day. July and early August had been wet, foreshortening the summer. However, Alan had assured me that Bulgaria would be hot, so I was dressed in a short skirt and a light, short-sleeved blouse.

As screens flickered above my head and in front of me, a girl decided to run down the aisle, her screaming mother in hot pursuit. An attractive flight attendant with an apparently permanent smile caught up with the girl then ushered mother and daughter to their seats, restoring order. We were moments from take-off – time to bite my fingernails, or dig them into the upholstery.

"Pavlina's looking forward to meeting you," Alan said, referring to his friend, Dr Pavlina Dimitrova, the conference organiser and our host for the next two weeks.

"Tell me about Pavlina; how did you meet her?"

"We met at a conference, in Canada, ten years ago."

"She's married, right?"

"For twenty years, to Petar, a history professor at Plovdiv University; they have a son, Mikhail, eighteen."

"Did Pavlina ever meet Elin?" I asked, referring to Alan's late wife.

"No." Alan shook his head sadly. "They never met. My friendship with Pavlina developed through international conferences and I only met her and Petar socially after Elin had died."

There was a sadness in Alan's voice whenever he spoke of Elin, and I sensed that he still missed her, that she'd left a big hole in his life. For some reason, beyond my comprehension, he'd fallen in love with me, a hot-headed mule with a troubled past. Maybe he saw me as an extension of his psychology practice. Maybe he felt sorry for me, and the physical abuse I'd suffered in the past. Or maybe, as he insisted, he was captivated by my beauty, enthralled by my sense of fun.

Fun was the last thing on my mind as the aeroplane moved beneath us and I pinned myself back, firmly in my seat. Too late to jump out now – we were on our way. As usual, when faced with fear, I felt the adrenaline flow into exhilaration. I offered Alan a tentative smile then, as the aeroplane left the ground, I thought, let's go for it, let's leave our cares behind, let's look forward to our holiday and see what the next fortnight might bring.

Chapter Two

Thankfully, the journey was a pleasant one, with no turbulence of any kind. After the ritual of customs, we met Dr Pavlina Dimitrova and her husband, Professor Petar Dimitrov, in the car park beside the glass-panelled airport at Plovdiv.

Petar was leaning against his car, a fresh from the showroom BMW, while Pavlina was smiling as she stepped forward to greet us. Short and petite, and in her mid-forties, Pavlina had dark, collar-length hair. Her eyes were dark, as black as midnight, and they contrasted sharply with her thin, pinched face, which despite the abundant sunshine was pallid and pale.

"Alan!" Pavlina embraced my fiancé then kissed him on both cheeks. "It is so nice to see you again." After taking a step back, she glanced in my direction, the smile still evident on her bright red lips. "And you must be Samantha." She appraised me through friendly, feminine eyes, one woman assessing another, with all the subconscious subplots such actions bring. "Alan's description and photographs do not do you justice; you are *very* beautiful."

"You are too kind." I blushed then glanced down to my sandals, suddenly aware of the stifling heat and the perspiration on my brow. Throughout my thirty-three years, I'd been fortunate to receive compliments; for some reason men, especially, found me attractive. However, emotionally scarred by my alcoholic mother and my violent ex-husband, I found it difficult to accept praise, though this character flaw was fading, thanks to Alan's love. To Pavlina, I smiled and said, "It's lovely to meet you."

"My husband, Petar." She nodded towards her spouse, a man blessed with dark hair, rippled with grey, dark eyes and a handsome, friendly face. Lean and standing around six foot tall, Petar exuded confidence and an affable sense of calm.

"Hello, Petar," I nodded while adjusting the strap on my travel bag.

"Hello, Samantha."

Petar took the travel bag from my hand and with Alan's help he placed our suitcases in the boot of his car.

As Alan heaved the largest and heaviest suitcase from the tarmac – mine, of course – he asked, "How's the vineyard, Petar?"

"His first question," Pavlina chided, "is about wine, not about me or my family."

"I'm sorry," Alan apologised profusely, "how are you, Pavlina? How's Mikhail?"

"I am well, a bit stressed about the conference, but now that you are here I am sure that everything will go fine. Mikhail is still behaving like a moody teenager. He is off to Sofia University soon and I am hopeful that the university will make a man of him."

"He needs a girlfriend," Petar mumbled, closing the boot of his car.

"He will find a girlfriend," Pavlina asserted confidently. "Maybe at the university."

As we climbed into the car – Petar and Pavlina on the front seats, Petar driving, Alan and yours truly on the back seats – Pavlina asked, "How is Alis?"

"She's fine," Alan replied. "She has her moody moments too but, like Mikhail, she'll soon set her sights on university, grades willing."

"She is not with you this time," Pavlina noted, her gaze wandering to the driver's mirror, her index finger removing an imaginary smudge from her left cheek.

"Alis is becoming more independent by the day. I think that's good for her. I think she's at an age now when she can stay on her own."

With the car windows open, offering a welcoming, cooling breeze, we pulled away from the airport and drove towards the city of Plovdiv.

We turned right, through a patchwork of fields; indeed, agriculture rolled before us as far as the eye could see. In the fields, I noticed wheat, onions, potatoes, tomatoes, barley and sugar beets all growing in abundance. As we travelled along a straight road, a red tractor shadowed us, ploughing a large, dry field while, to my left, I spied a weary horse, a herd of suspicious cows and some frisky goats.

"You were asking about the wine," Petar said, his attention on the road as he eased past a young woman, riding a horse.

"Yes," Alan replied, "how is the vineyard?"

"Flourishing. We had a good crop last year and this year will be even better. When we get to Grozdovo, you must sample the wine."

"But not too much," I cautioned.

"There's no drinking water at Petar's holiday home," Alan explained, "and we have to imbibe something, so why not the wine?"

"I'm sure Pavlina has plenty of bottled water," I reasoned.

"Ignore them." Pavlina glanced over her shoulder. She smiled, "Men become children when they talk of their favourite things."

"You are my favourite thing, my sweetie," Petar grinned while patting his wife's thigh.

"Now he is being facetious," Pavlina scowled, though the twinkle in her eyes revealed that she did appreciate her husband's words and gesture.

As we entered the city of Plovdiv, the grey

residential and industrial buildings offered a sharp contrast to the fertile fields, now fading into the distance. I've never been an admirer of tower blocks and the tower blocks of Plovdiv, legacies of the communist era, did little to change my mind – drab and dreary, they looked ripe for the wrecking ball. However, travelling through the city, a sports centre seemed fresh and modern while the hotels appeared hospitable. Dating from the 1800s, another rise of apartments offered a more attractive facade with their colourful paintwork and ornate balconies while an area of parkland provided a splash of verdant green.

Then, with the sun beating down and my skirt sticking to the car seat, we travelled through a residential neighbourhood, the neat semi-detached buildings all distinguished by bright terracotta roofs.

On the outskirts of Plovdiv the houses thinned and soon we were into the countryside again, passing through fields awash with lavender, roses, poppies and sunflowers, dotted with apple and pear trees all bearing succulent fruit.

"How's Irena?" Alan asked while my eyes feasted on the fruit.

"My mother...," Pavlina offered a gentle shrug of her slender shoulders, "she is in her eighties, yet she still insists on running the home. She will cook and sew and tend the garden from sunrise until sundown, if you let her."

"Which Pavlina does," Petar mumbled, *sotto voce*.

"Petar exaggerates." Pavlina turned towards her husband and offered him a censorious frown. "But," she continued, her tone now light and joyful, "it is good for my mother to be active; it keeps her young in body and spirit."

We travelled on, through more countryside. Then, while glancing through the open car window, I observed, "The fields are full of beautiful flowers."

"The roses," Petar smiled. He slowed at a junction and took the opportunity to stretch his arms and back by pushing against the steering wheel. "Bulgaria produces over seventy percent of the world's attar, the extract of roses, the oil for making perfume. Perfumeries spend a fortune on our attar. Our attar is worth more than gold on some markets! Each acre planted produces around three million rosebuds and from the attar the residue of rosewater and pulp is used to make jams, medicines and liqueurs."

From the rose fields, we travelled west, the road skirting the village of Kadievo before winding through open countryside again, reaching the village of Mir. At Mir, we turned south, through more agriculture, eventually arriving at another village, Perushtitsa. Then we climbed, off the main roads on to dirt tracks, snaking our way up the mountain through a lush panoply of green trees.

The fresh scent of the forest teased my nostrils while the uneven, twisty road jiggled my stomach. The combination of fragrant air and bumpy road produced a strange sensation, a sensation that matched my mood and the contradictory thoughts running through my mind; I was excited and looking forward to the holiday, yet missing my office and my home.

After an hour and twenty minutes all told, we arrived at our destination. With a sense of relief, I climbed out of the car and smiled at Petar. He returned my smile then announced proudly, "Welcome to Grozdovo! Welcome to our holiday home!"

Chapter Three

Petar opened a pair of iron gates then parked his
BMW on an area of gravel. The gravelled area could
accommodate four cars, no trouble, though only a
bright blue Fiesta, presumably Pavlina's, was in
residence. Beside the gravel, I spied a lawn, brown
from the summer sun, and a small swimming pool,
its lining pale blue, its outer shell a neat patchwork
of large, irregular stones. A water feature, a large
pond covered with lilies, occupied the north corner
of the garden while a small fountain rose from this
feature, splashing water on to the goldfish,
threatening to soak a swarm of buzzing bees.

Petar's holiday home was one of twenty
scattered on the hillside. Most were hidden, though
some were visible through the gaps in the trees. The
house itself was a single storey, long and white with
three small chimneys protruding through the roof.
A satellite dish offered evidence of the twenty-first
century, though the air of peace and tranquillity
transported you back to another time.

"What a lovely place," I sighed, suddenly
feeling languid and rested.

"All built with my own fair hands," Petar
grinned while dragging my suitcase from his car.

"And the hands of friends," Pavlina added, her

fingers easing a gold chain away from a small mole at the nape of her neck, placing the jewellery on her variegated blouse. "It has taken us ten years to get the house looking like this, but it has been worth the effort; we are very proud of it."

I nodded. It was a lovely house and they had every right to feel proud.

Between us, we placed the suitcases in the house then Petar grabbed Alan's arm. He winked, mischievously. "The vineyard..."

I followed Petar and Alan to the rear of the house where they admired row upon row of green and red grapes dangling, invitingly, from metal frames.

Petar plucked a handful of grapes, washed them with bottled water then offered them to us. Needless to say, we sampled the grapes and discovered that they were very tasty.

"Excellent," Alan announced while accepting a second serving of grapes.

"The grapes are fine, but wait until you taste the wine...," Petar pursed his lips, as though savouring the nectar, "delightful. Worry not, my friend, you will sample my labours later."

I have a low alcohol threshold and the thought of Petar's wine alone was enough to induce a hangover. However, before my mind could run away with that thought, a young man appeared in the garden, having walked in from the forest. Dressed in an athletic vest, shorts and running shoes, he had dark hair, cut short, dark eyes and a handsome, unblemished face. Standing well over six foot tall, he possessed a muscular physique, a physique to match his sporting attire. Indeed, he was a youthful Adonis who would turn the heads of many a female before he was much older. However, despite his impressive natural attributes, he was somewhat shy, lingering by the swimming pool, not daring to venture towards us.

"Ah, Mikhail." Pavlina walked towards the youth. At first, he was reluctant then with a shrug he acquiesced, joining his mother at our side. "This is our son, Mikhail. Alan, you know. This is Samantha."

"Hi," I said brightly.

"Hello," Mikhail frowned, his eyes staring at the stony ground.

Before I could reply further, an elderly woman, in her mid-eighties, emerged from the house. Standing around five foot tall and wearing an embroidered apron, the lady had grey hair, pulled back into a bun, brown beguiling eyes and a face surprisingly free of wrinkles. Her erect posture, along with her face, belied her mature age.

"And this is my mother, Irena." Pavlina took hold of Irena's elbow and guided her towards us.

"My mother has no English," Pavlina explained, "but I will translate."

"Zdraveite; hello," I said, offering my phrasebook Bulgarian.

Irena giggled at my mangling of the native language. Then she enveloped me in a big, warm hug. With some people, you click instantly and from that moment on, I knew that we'd be friends.

Irena talked with Pavlina in rapid Bulgarian. Then Pavlina turned to us ready to translate. "My mother says dinner will be served in an hour. Maybe you would like to freshen up first. I will show you to your room."

We followed Pavlina into a spacious bedroom equipped with a large double bed. We unpacked quickly, placing our clothes in a wardrobe and a chest of drawers, then I decamped to the shower to wash the sweat from my pores. The water was incredibly hot and I recalled Alan's words telling me that Petar had rigged a container, painted black, which stored the water for the shower and for washing. In the summer, the sun heated the water, to scalding point.

After the shower, I slipped into a light summer frock, a floral creation, the type I'd wear on holiday, but wouldn't be seen dead in at home; you see, I'm not a 'pink' girl, I prefer darker and autumnal hues. But when in Rome...or when in Bulgaria for that matter...

At 8 p.m., dinner was served and I joined Alan and our hosts at the dining table, a large oak affair covered in a fine, lace tablecloth.

Pavlina placed white, china plates before us while Petar produced the wine glasses and the wine. Then Irena appeared, carrying a large tureen, crammed with salad.

"That looks and smells yummy," I said as Mikhail dragged a chair away from the table and sat opposite me.

"It's a shepherds' salad," Pavlina explained: "tomatoes, cucumbers, mushrooms, peppers, onions, eggs, drizzled with olive oil and vinegar and sprinkled with feta cheese."

"Alan informed us that you are a vegetarian," Petar added, "so Irena prepared a vegetarian dish, in your honour."

I shrugged modestly and bit my lower lip. "You shouldn't have gone to all that trouble."

"Don't worry," Petar grinned, "I am preparing a barbeque tomorrow; there will be plenty of meat around for us carnivores."

Irena joined us at the dinner table while Petar served the wine, pouring generous measures into tall glasses. We loaded our plates with salad, sipped the wine then, in appreciative silence, enjoyed our meal.

"Please tell your mother," I said while dabbing my lips with a napkin, "this is delicious."

Pavlina turned to Irena and translated. The matriarch smiled then shook her head.

"My mother thanks you," Pavlina said.

The frown on my forehead must have betrayed my confusion because Petar set his wine glass on the table and explained: "You are wondering why Irena shook her head instead of nodding. It is common in Greece and Albania too. We move our heads in the wrong direction. There is no logical explanation, though some people think the gesture dates back to the Ottoman Empire and religious practices in the sixteenth century."

I nodded then wondered if I should have wobbled my head. Sensing my dilemma, Irena smiled.

After devouring a second helping of the shepherds' salad, Alan asked, "How are preparations going for the conference?"

"Well," Pavlina replied. She ate slowly, I noted, lifting modest forkfuls from her small plate. "Now that you are here, all the principal speakers have arrived."

Alan arched an eyebrow then sipped his wine. "Including Dr Stine?"

"Otto is here." Pavlina dabbed her lips with a napkin then emitted a playful laugh. "And I know how much you will love his lecture."

Softly, Alan groaned, hinting at his displeasure. "Stine is a clever man, but he's convinced himself that he knows all the answers; he's too clever for his own good."

Pavlina extended her long, slender fingers displaying her palm, a defensive gesture stating 'what can you do?' She added, "He is pompous, I agree. But a diversity of opinion should help to stimulate debate."

From over the rim of his wine glass, Petar asked, "And while they are talking, Samantha, what will you do?"

"I thought I'd have a look around; play the tourist. Maybe hire a car..."

Petar nodded, in western style. Instinctively, I glanced towards Irena; Pavlina claimed that her mother had no English, yet her dancing eyes and occasional smiles suggested that she was following the gist of our conversation.

"I will arrange a hire car for you," Petar said. "But you will need a guide."

"Mikhail is free," Pavlina added. The last to finish, she'd emptied her plate.

"Indeed he is," Petar mused while reaching for another bottle of wine. "What about it, Mikhail, will you play host to our guest?"

Quiet throughout the meal, Mikhail stared at

the lace tablecloth. He mumbled then offered a diffident shrug. "I suppose so."

"Splendid," Petar enthused. He stood and poured a fresh measure of wine into each wine glass. "I will arrange the hire car in the morning."

We sipped our wine. Then we sampled our dessert, a delicious dish of baked apples crammed with walnuts, raisins and cinnamon. A generous helping of vanilla ice cream added to the delight and, although already stuffed, I consented to a second serving.

We chatted amiably, sharing jokes, opinions, recollections. In an effort to draw Irena into the conversation, I said, "Alan has told me many good things about Pavlina. You must be very proud to be the mother of such an intelligent daughter."

Irena said something to Pavlina in Bulgarian then sat back in her chair and laughed.

"Mother!" Pavlina scowled. "You can't say that!"

While smiling quietly to himself, Petar offered a translation, "Irena said that Pavlina is her 'little miracle'. It took Irena forty-one years to produce a child, but she had plenty of fun trying!"

Pavlina's cheeks coloured, turning scarlet. She stared at her fingers, which were resting on the tablecloth. "Don't encourage her, Petar; you are embarrassing our guests."

Petar shrugged. He rolled his eyes then hid his jovial features behind his wine glass. "Samantha is a private detective; I am sure that it will take a lot to embarrass her."

I thought back to earlier misadventures; to a pimp called Blade and his naked form, wandering through the mists of Cardiff; to a hit man called George Kosminski and his bare backside: George was into sadistic bondage sessions and, on one occasion, I'd interviewed him when he was so chained. Recalling those moments and more, I sighed, "Yeah, I've seen some sights in my time."

Our dinner complete, we wandered into the living room, a large space decorated with pine panels on the walls. As I sat in an armchair, I allowed my eyes to wander, to a line of yoga DVDs positioned near the piano. Probably, Pavlina owned the DVDs and she played the piano; she had long fingers, ideally suited to the instrument and the mildly neurotic air that pianists tend to exude.

A pile of history books and Dire Straits CDs atop a laptop computer would belong to Petar while the modern music CDs, the football magazines, the graphic novels and the fitness books would belong to Mikhail. A rocking chair, its arms and legs well worn, and a low table highlighted Irena's presence in the room. An old radio sat on the table beside a sewing kit and a well-thumbed novel, *Fathers and*

Children by Ivan Turgenev.

Next, a collection of old photographs caught my eye. I stood, walked to the south wall and examined the photographs. One of the pictures, a sepia image from the 1940s, was very appealing. The image portrayed a family of fifteen, great-grandparents, grandparents, parents and children. Two people in particular stood out – a young girl and a handsome man with an Errol Flynn moustache. The man wore a military uniform, buttoned to the neck, and a soft, flat hat. A cigarette dangled from his left hand while his smile hinted at warmth.

Turning to Irena, I said, "That's a lovely photograph. The young girl...is that you?"

Breaking away from Mikhail, Pavlina stepped forward and answered for her mother. "Yes, that is Irena, aged nine."

"And the man at her side?"

Pavlina averted her eyes. Bowing her head, she stared at the circular pattern on the carpet. "We don't talk about him anymore."

"Why not?" I asked.

Now, Petar stepped forward, placing his wine glass on the piano. While staring at the picture, he said, "That man is Emil Angelov, Irena's father. During the Second World War, Emil fought for the communists against the fascists, alongside his comrades, the men of Mir. One night, in the forest, there was a great slaughter. The men of Mir had been lured to the forest, where the fascists were waiting. Emil was captured and later released. He had betrayed his comrades to the fascists and was released as a gesture of thanks. Upon his release, Emil returned to Mir, but everyone ignored him. In disgrace, he left the village and went to live to the north of Plovdiv, in Hisarya, as a hermit. The community shunned Irena and her mother, so they left Mir to settle in Plovdiv. Every family in Mir was touched by the slaughter. The fascists murdered a generation of men in one night. Time heals, yes, but nerves are still raw, even today. Irena is her father's daughter and she carries his disgrace. That is why no one talks of Emil, even to this day."

"What became of Emil?" I asked.

"When the communists seized power, towards the end of the war, the womenfolk told them of Emil's betrayal. As with many traitors, the communists conducted a swift trial, pronounced Emil guilty then took him into the forest, where they shot him, dead."

I glanced at Irena and noticed that her brown eyes were brimming with tears. To the matriarch, I apologised, "I am sorry, Irena. I am sorry I raised the subject."

"No," Petar insisted, hoisting his glass and

drinking a soupcon of wine, "it is good to talk. It is time to talk. We have tiptoed around the past for too long."

After listening intently to the conversation, Alan walked over and stood at my side. He placed an arm around my shoulders, hugged me and said, "It's been a long day; I think we'd better hit the hay."

Pavlina nodded. Maybe it was the strain of the conference, Emil's story, or her natural demeanour, but she looked tired. She managed a polite smile then said, "I wish you goodnight."

"Goodnight," I replied. Then turning to Irena, I repeated, "Goodnight."

"Leka nosht," Irena said. Then she walked out of the room, to dry her eyes.

Chapter Four

As usual, I was the last one out of bed – even at the best of times I am not a morning person. The night, pitch-black save for the moon, had been quiet despite the chirping of the crickets. Although Petar and Pavlina had placed shutters on the windows along with lace curtains, the mosquitoes had still got through and feasted on my flesh.

I showered, adding a generous amount of cold water to the supply from Petar's natural boiler, then read Alan's note, propped against my perfume: Petar had arranged a hire car and would spend the day at the university, preparing for the new term; Alan and Pavlina would also be at the university, attending the conference; Mikhail would act as my guide and would take me anywhere I wanted to go.

But first, breakfast, which consisted of kifla – a bread roll with marmalade – coffee and fruit juice.

After breakfast, I found Irena in the garden, tending her roses. We exchanged a cheerful 'dobro utro' – 'good morning' – then I sat on the patio, admiring the view. Below me stretched the green fields and vineyards of the Trakia Valley, while the Rhodope Mountains rose majestically and craggily towards the light, fluffy clouds. Irena seemed her old ebullient self this morning, the memory of Emil and his betrayal apparently forgotten, assuming that you can forget a memory that's been with you for over seventy years.

I switched on my phone and discovered that I had a stream of messages from my old friend, Detective Inspector 'Sweets' MacArthur. The messages amounted to a joke: It's the Cold War and three men are sitting in a Bulgarian café. One of the men glances at a newspaper, shakes his head and sighs. The second man looks at his newspaper, shakes his head and sighs. Annoyed, the third man reaches for his hat and coat and says, 'If you two are going to discuss politics, I'm off.'

I smiled, quietly to myself and wondered what my hosts would make of the joke. Maybe I'd share it with them, one day; and discuss daily life during the days of Communism.

Grozdovo was situated high on the hillside so I had no trouble obtaining an Internet connection. As previously arranged, I made a video call to my friend, Faye.

After a brief lull, Faye flickered into life and I gazed at her smiling face.

"Hiya," she said cheerily.

"Hi. How are things at home?"

"Okay. No probs."

"How's Marlowe?"

Faye angled her computer and Marlowe came

into view. As usual, he was curled up on my desk, sound asleep. "He spent yesterday morning meowing," Faye informed me, "because you weren't around. But he's settled down now."

"Don't over-feed him."

Once again, Faye came into view, and so did her scowl. "I won't."

"How's the office?"

"Fine."

"Any calls?"

"Routine." Faye pushed out her bottom lip. She shrugged. "Nothing I can't handle."

"If anything important comes along, get in touch."

"Sam," she admonished, "you're on holiday."

"I know, but..."

"But you don't trust me, right?"

As though unaware that she was on camera, Faye started to tidy the items on my desk. The items were neat enough in the first place, but Faye's fingers were busy, her default reaction when she felt under stress.

"Of course I trust you," I insisted.

"Uh-huh." She nodded, thought for a while, offered a brief smile then sat back, placated. "I've been systematizing your files."

"Faye..."

"Don't worry..." Again the scowl and the busy

fingers. "I won't pry. I know your files are confidential, but I'm introducing a new system. When you get back, you'll see; it'll be heaps better, more efficient." She swayed out of shot for a moment; when she returned, her generous lips were swathed in a big smile. "What are you up to?"

"I'm off sightseeing now."

"Anywhere nice?"

"Plovdiv old town."

"Oh, right." Absentmindedly, Faye tugged at her golden ringlets, playing with her hair. "What are the men like out there?"

"What do you mean?" I frowned. "What are they like?"

"Are they hunky?" Faye replied, offering a wicked grin.

"Some are good looking, yeah."

"Bet it's hot there."

"Roasting."

"You gone topless yet?"

"Faye," I admonished, "I'm staying with a family and their eighteen-year-old son."

"Oh," she wrinkled her dainty nose, "that must cramp your style. Better stay covered up then; you don't want to give anyone the wrong impression, do ya? Don't want to give anyone any wrong ideas."

Faye was ten years younger than me and,

sometimes, I thought the age difference showed.

I adjusted my phone and shook my head. "You have a filthy mind, do you know that?"

She laughed, out loud and vulgar. Then she poked out her tongue. "Takes one to know one. Have fun. See ya!"

And to this woman I'd entrusted my professional career...She was a decent, conscientious person; she wouldn't screw anything up – would she?

While I was pondering that point, Mikhail appeared on the patio. "Are you ready?" he asked.

"Yeah."

"Okay; let's go."

I gathered my shoulder bag from the bedroom, said 'bye' to Irena then jumped into the hire car, a Suzuki Alto. The car was left-hand drive, which took a bit of getting used to, but as we weaved our way down the mountain road, parallel to a canal, I found myself slipping through the gears.

The road took us through Perushtitsa, Mir and Kadievo and, as we travelled, I observed, "There are many buses on the streets."

Mikhail nodded. Dressed in a fresh pair of shorts and a sports vest, he seemed more at ease in my company today. "It's a good way to get around. Buses are more reliable and quicker than trains in Bulgaria."

"You're off to university soon."

Again, he nodded, "Yeah."

"To Sofia."

"Yeah."

"Are you looking forward to it?"

This time, he shrugged, "I guess so."

"What will you study there?"

"Archaeology."

I smiled while checking my rear-view mirror. I noted that most of the cars were modern, though a few Moscovich's were still clunking around. "You're following in your father's footsteps; you're into the past."

Again, a diffident shrug. "I guess so."

We arrived in Plovdiv and I parked the car. Like Mikhail, I was wearing shorts, and a halter-neck top, which clung to my curves. I couldn't help noticing that Mikhail was admiring my curves. Maybe to distract him, maybe to cool down, I suggested, "Let's buy an ice cream."

We walked down a cobbled street, licking our ice creams. Along the way, we passed a golden domed cathedral and the Academy of Music, Dance and Fine Arts. I was glancing to my left, to the City Art Gallery, when Mikhail said, "Do you want to see the Ancient Theatre?"

I nodded and smiled. "I'd love to."

So we turned right and walked a short distance

along another cobbled street. The sun was beating down, baking the cobbles, threatening to melt the soles on my shoes.

"This is the Ancient Theatre," Mikhail announced and I stood in awe, admiring the ornate columns and the stone sculptures, the sense of grandeur and the magnificent craftsmanship of the partial ruin. "The theatre was built around the first or second century. It seated over 6,000 spectators and was a popular venue until the fifth century when it was destroyed by fire or an earthquake. Today, it is a symbol of the modern town. You probably know that Plovdiv is one of the oldest cities in Europe. Plovdiv is as old as Troy, and older than Athens and Rome. The Thracians were the first to settle here; they called the place Evmolpia. In the fourth century, Philip of Macedon conquered the city. He built a wall around it and the name changed to Philippopolis. Then in 1364 the Ottomans invaded and the names changed again, along with the architecture, of course." Although Mikhail was talking about the Ancient Theatre, his eyes were firmly fixed on me. When I turned to meet his gaze, he looked away, ducking his head somewhat shyly. "Do you want to see the Roman Stadium?" he mumbled.

I nodded. "I'd love to."

We strolled past the Church of St Marina and

an exhibition gallery, side-stepping a knot of eager Japanese tourists, their cameras at the ready. At the Roman Stadium, an impressive open amphitheatre surrounded by banked stone seating, Mikhail said, "The stadium was built in the second century, a copy of the Delphi stadium. Only twelve antique constructions of this type exist in the whole world. The stadium seated 30,000 spectators, so was like a modern football ground. Do you like football?"

I shook my head and frowned. "I'm not a sporty type."

"Oh." Mikhail leaned against the glass barrier and continued, "Gladiators fought here, against animals..."

"I think I prefer football."

"...and the marble seats for the spectators are well preserved, as you can see."

From the Roman Stadium we strolled south, along a wide street bearing the name Knyaz Aleksandar I. Pausing outside a gift shop, I said, "I'd better buy something for my friend, Faye. What do you recommend?"

"Fur hats are popular, or maybe a tee-shirt with Putin?"

I pulled a face and scowled. "I think not."

"Rose oil is nice," Mikhail suggested helpfully, "or a copper pot for tea? Or a wood carving, or a handmade blanket?"

I studied the gift shop through its window, flicked my hair from my perspiring back and made a decision. "I think a warm hat for our winter snow and some rose oil would be nice."

"Good choice," Mikhail approved, and I disappeared into the gift shop to make my purchases. In the gift shop I also bought a hat for myself, a flouncy, wide-brimmed number; if you're going to play the tourist, you might as well go the whole hog.

As I emerged, tying my long auburn hair into a ponytail, adjusting the hat on the crown of my head, Mikhail asked, "Do you want to see the dig near the Forum and Odeon?"

"Yes, please."

We continued south, through narrow winding streets, glancing at brightly painted buildings, buildings that leaned towards each other, threatening to touch. Some of the buildings were occupied while others were museum pieces, a combination of the past and present, of the ancient and modern. Trees lined the streets, breaking through the cobblestones, which were irregular and large, while the glass-panelled street lamps offered a Victorian air.

Eventually, we arrived at a large square and the Central Post Office. Beside the Post Office, we spied additional ancient remains and evidence of an archaeological dig.

While I studied the stone steps and foundations exposed by the dig, Mikhail said, "This dig complements the Forum and Odeon. The Forum was erected during the time of Vespasian, in the years A.D. 69 – 79, and later modernised. It contained many shops and public buildings. The Odeon was built in the second century and functioned until the fifth century. It seated around 500 people. Concerts are sometimes held there."

As I gazed at the archaeological remains my mind went racing through the centuries, back to Roman times; I could picture the centurions, sweating in their heavy armour, marching through the cobbled streets.

"This place is so fascinating," I said; "it's loaded with history."

"Yeah." Mikhail stared at his trainers; he shuffled his feet. From the corner of his eye, he offered me a bashful look. "Where do you wanna go now?"

"I've been thinking about Emil...can we go to Hisarya?"

"This afternoon?"

"Why not?"

"Okay," Mikhail nodded. He stepped past me then paused to glance over his shoulder. "You're very pretty, Samantha; I hope you don't mind me saying that. Come on," he added hastily, "let's go to Hisarya; I'll guide you there."

Chapter Five

We travelled north, away from the old town of Plovdiv, across the green water of the Maritsa River into a region of industry and agriculture.

At one point, near the village of Trud, we encountered an interesting road configuration – two figures of eight set within a diamond. Thankfully, the road to Hisarya went straight through the figures of eight and the diamond so my driving and navigation skills were not put to the test.

After Trud, we passed through the occasional village; small settlements scattered within the vast expanse of brown and green countryside. In one of the villages, Duvanlii, I noticed an abundance of red and white bracelets hanging from roadside trees. I asked Mikhail about the bracelets. "What do they symbolise?"

"I think it's a pagan tradition. They are called Martenitsa. The red and white thread of the bracelets represents male and female, and we present the Martenitsa to our family and friends on the first of March."

"Our St David's Day," I smiled.

Mikhail turned to look at me then resumed his pose, staring out of the side window. "The bracelets offer health for the new year to come. That's why I think it's a pagan ritual, because the New Year is when the earth awakens and people start work in the fields. March is the month of Baba Marta – Grandma March – the Great Mother Goddess and the oldest woman in the family of months. We wear the Martenitsa until we see a stork or blossoms on the trees. Then we transfer the Martenitsa to the trees, to ask for good health and for the land to bear us fruit."

From Duvanlii we passed through kilometre after kilometre of agriculture until, forty kilometres into our journey, we arrived at Hisarya.

I drove slowly through the town, absorbing the surroundings. From the corner of my eye, I noted that Mikhail was admiring my thighs. However, when I glanced in his direction, hurriedly he looked away.

In the sunshine, the temperature touched forty degrees Celsius and I was wilting with the heat. So I parked the car and we walked in the shade, under a canopy of tall, broadleaved trees.

As we ambled along a country lane, Mikhail said, "You will notice that Hisarya is surrounded by forest. In fact, there are hundreds of acres of parkland within the vicinity. Hisarya is famous for its mineral springs; there are twenty-two of them. The water is lightly mineralised – alkaline, hydro-carbonate-sodium and fluorine. The springs are mildly radioactive and their temperature can reach fifty degrees Celsius. The water is good for kidney, urological, gastric, intestinal and liver disorders, and now it's bottled and sold to locals and tourists. The Romans were the first to utilise the mineral water." He paused then added, "Would you like to see the south gate?"

I smiled and nodded, "I'd love to."

Keeping to the shade, we made our leisurely way along the country lanes to a large stone arch, topped with the remnants of a further stone structure. The arch contained a patchwork of orange and brown stones, dappled with green vegetation.

"This gate is known as 'The Camels'," Mikhail explained, "because people think it looks like two camels facing each other. What do you think?"

The protruding columns looked like horns to me, but I conceded, "They have a point."

"The gate was partially restored about a hundred years ago."

I nodded then asked, "Where did the hermit live?"

"Not here." Mikhail turned and pointed towards the east. "He lived outside the town. Shall I show you?"

"Yes, please."

We returned to the hire car and travelled through the town, along attractive tree-lined streets, past tall multi-layered walls, remnants of the Roman occupation. Glancing to my left and right I spied a number of large hotels with sport, spa and recreational facilities, along with smaller hotels and guest houses. Two thousand years had passed, but Hisarya remained as a health and leisure resort.

We drove a few kilometres east, out of the spa town into a region of sylvan beauty, dominated by tall, green trees. Within a clearing, and with birdsong filling our ears, we found a spring and beside the spring the remains of a small stone shack.

"This is where the hermit used to live," Mikhail explained; "this is his cell."

The shack was no more than one room, devoid of its roof now and with its walls robbed down to hip level. I gazed at the shack, at a range of stone shelves, at the remnants of a primitive fireplace and asked, "What do you know about Emil?"

"Nothing, really. Only that he betrayed the people of Mir and that we no longer talk about him."

"The people of Mir are still upset by what happened?"

"The people of Mir are country people. The past matters to them. Their memories run deep."

I nodded. I could understand and accept that. Although born and raised in a modern city, I respected tradition and those who cherished the past. While squatting and running my fingers over the broken stones, I asked, "Only Emil escaped the massacre?"

"And a handful of others; but they are dead now."

"All of them?"

Mikhail paused. He frowned then said, "Except for Ivan."

"Ivan?"

"Ivan Simeonov. He was one of the Resistance fighters against the fascists."

"Fascinating." I stood and brushed the dust from my hands. While fanning my face with my recently acquired hat, I asked, "Can we talk with Ivan?"

"He still lives in Mir. I'll ask."

I plonked the hat on my head, at a suitably rakish angle then followed Mikhail from the clearing, back to the hire car.

As we walked, Mikhail slowed then turned and said, "Samantha..."

"Yes?"

"You are engaged to Dr Storey."

"Yes."

"Does he love you?"

"I think he does."

"Do you love him?"

"I do," I replied with a smile. Then I frowned.

"Why do you ask?"

Mikhail shrugged. He walked ahead. "No reason."

Chapter Six

The light was fading as we arrived back at Petar's house. I parked the car, climbed out and watched in thoughtful silence as Mikhail disappeared into the building.

Then my spirits lifted when Alan appeared on the patio. He walked over to me, stooped slightly, kissed me and said, "We'd given you up for lost." I allowed his kiss to linger, my chin resting against his finely trimmed goatee beard, his right hand playfully tapping my behind. As he slipped my arm through his, he asked, "Had an enjoyable day?"

"Yes, a very enjoyable day." I told Alan about our trip to the old town and our visit to Hisarya. "I hope to talk with Ivan Simeonov tomorrow," I said as Pavlina joined us on the patio. Noting the frown on Pavlina's forehead, I added, "I hope you don't mind, Pavlina?"

"No, I don't mind," she said hastily. Then, after a deep breath and a sigh to compose herself, she added, "As Petar says, it is time we talked about my grandfather; we need to be more open about the past."

Under Alan's pensive gaze, Pavlina retreated to the house. After caressing his chin and nodding quietly to himself he turned to me and said,

"Careful whose toes you tread on; remember – you're in a foreign country; Sweets isn't around."

I glanced up at Alan and smiled sweetly. "I won't tread on any toes. I'll be diplomatic and careful, just as I am at home."

"Hmm," he mumbled, noncommittally. Then he turned his attention to Pavlina, who'd emerged from the house carrying a tray crammed with meat: sausages, chicken and lamb.

Pavlina walked over to Petar. Her husband was sitting at the side of the house, beside a fireplace built against an outside wall. The fireplace contained the barbeque and with string bags stuffed with daffodil bulbs hanging above his head, Petar stoked the fire, adding more meat.

"Tell me about the conference," I said while hopping over a ground-level vine offering the prospect of wine in years to come. Along with Alan, I sat on a wooden chair, on the patio.

"The conference got off to a...er...interesting start."

"In other words, Alan found Dr Stine's talk disagreeable," Pavlina said with a smile. Having divested herself of the meat tray, now she was arranging cutlery and plates on a long, pine picnic table.

"Not disagreeable," Alan said, "though I would argue with many of his outdated Freudian concepts."

"You Humanists are all the same," Pavlina insisted, "you regard Freud's theories as negative, deterministic and demeaning. Never mind," she added with a smile, "you can make your points tomorrow and Dr Stine can disagree with you."

"Ask ten psychologists for an opinion and you will receive ten different answers," Petar chipped in while leaning back on his stool and mopping his brow.

"Psychology is a complex subject and often a matter of opinion," Pavlina asserted with a serious frown. "That is why these conferences are so valuable; opinions can be shared, minds can be opened and people can be introduced to fresh ideas and concepts."

"True," Alan agreed. Then he added with a mischievous wink, "But I still say Dr Stine's ideas are outdated."

"Enough talk." Pavlina waved a hand in dismissive fashion; "let's eat."

"But first a drink," Petar insisted, leaning forward, reaching for a bottle of wine.

"But first a shower," I pleaded, waving my hat as a fan.

"Okay," Petar conceded, "you shower, then a drink."

I slipped out of my sweaty clothes, had a cool

shower, then dressed in a modest summer smock; time to cover up my bare skin, which had burnt under the hot afternoon sun.

As I resumed my seat on the patio, Petar approached with a bottle and a small glass in his hands. "What's that?" I asked as he poured the alcohol into the glass.

"Rakia; made from grapes from our vineyard."

"I should warn you," Pavlina added, her words heavy with caution, "our Rakia is very potent indeed."

"And I should warn you," I frowned, "that I have a very low alcohol threshold."

"All the better for the karaoke later," Petar insisted while topping up my already full glass, "my Rakia will make you sing."

I sipped the Rakia cautiously then glanced at Alan. "Karaoke?"

In turn, Alan sipped his Rakia. He offered a playful shrug. "It's a family tradition."

Along with the Rakia and meat for the carnivores, we enjoyed a tasty Shopska salad – tomatoes, cucumbers, green peppers, onions and feta cheese all drizzled with red vinegar wine and olive oil.

We were chatting pleasantly – myself, Alan, Pavlina, Petar, Irena and Mikhail – when a man appeared at the front gate carrying a plastic shopping bag. In his early fifties with a lugubrious air, the man had short, wavy hair, predominantly grey, dark, intense eyes and a leonine face. As he approached, I noticed that his chin and cheeks were swathed in a dark five o'clock shadow. Of average height and medium build, he carried a slight paunch and wore, on his left hand, a wedding ring.

"Ah, Vasil...," Petar stood to greet the man, "come and join us...a glass of Rakia?"

"Just a small one," Vasil insisted, indicating the measure with his index finger and thumb.

"This is Vasil Petrov, a neighbour," Petar explained. "Vasil is building a country house near that clearing. He is a detective in the Plovdiv police."

I nodded and smiled. "Pleased to meet you."

"This is Dr Alan Storey," Petar said to Detective Petrov.

"We met," Alan said; he stood and shook the detective's hand, "briefly, on my previous trip."

"I remember," Petrov said while stroking his chin.

"And his fiancée, Samantha," Petar continued. "Samantha is also a detective, a private eye."

"Like Sam Spade," Petrov said. I sensed that it would take a lot to make Petrov smile, but he almost grinned.

"Without the falcon," I replied, my lips sipping

the Rakia.

"I am pleased to meet you," Petrov bowed graciously. To Petar, he added, "I only called to return your drill." He held up the plastic shopping bag. "I have bought a new one..."

"Vasil burned out his drill bolting together some rafters," Petar explained. "He is building a beautiful house."

"It will be beautiful," Petrov agreed, his tone laced with caution, "when it is finished."

"That will be soon," Petar stated confidently. "Vasil is very dogged and persistent; that is why the criminals fear him so much; and that is why he will complete his house – he always gets the job done."

Petrov tilted his head back and consumed his Rakia. "I should not impose myself any longer," he insisted, placing his glass and shopping bag on the picnic table. He inclined his head towards me and said, "It has been a pleasure to meet you."

"Alan and Samantha are staying for a fortnight," Petar explained. "Call again, soon."

Petrov nodded. "If time and the criminal fraternity allow, I will."

Petar placed the drill in his house then emerged carrying a small karaoke machine and a beautifully crafted, antique guitar. "Music time!" he announced with a grin.

As everyone lapsed into joyful small talk, I

recalled my schooldays and the school choir. My angelic looks had ushered me into Mr Hughes' choir while, after one singing lesson, my voice had thrust me out. Think of Monty Python's Mr Gumby playing an out-of-tune violin and you'll have some idea of my musical 'ability'.

"I should warn you now," I cautioned, "I can't sing."

"But you are Welsh," Pavlina noted; "it is famous; all Welsh people can sing."

I shrugged, apologetically, "I'm the exception that proves the rule."

"Honestly," Alan said, leaning towards Pavlina, "she has a terrible singing voice; she can't sing."

"Here," Petar insisted, loading my glass with yet more Rakia, "have another sip of this and you will sing like an angel."

"I will," I said, referring to the Rakia, "but I won't," I added, recalling my voice.

The music started and Petar took to the stage, or rather the patio, with an over-the-top rendition of Elton John's 'Crocodile Rock'. Through the laughter and Rakia, we joined in with the la-la-la-la-la's.

After applauding her husband, Pavlina turned to me and said, "Many people of the 1960s, 1970s and 1980s generations learned their English from pop songs."

I nodded and replied in admiration, "You all speak excellent English."

"Here...," Petar was at the bottle again and topping up my glass, "have another slurp of Rakia and soon you'll be talking Bulgarian."

I sipped then gulped the Rakia. In a thick, slurry voice, a voice I barely recognised as my own, I said to Alan, "He's trying to get me pissed."

"Darling," Alan replied, offering a kiss to my left cheek, "he's no longer trying; he's succeeded."

"Your turn, Mikhail," Pavlina said, jumping up, clearly enjoying the occasion.

Quiet throughout the barbeque, Mikhail dipped his head and sighed, "I don't want to."

"Come on," his mother chided, "don't be a spoilsport."

Scowling at Mikhail, Irena said something in Bulgarian and, reluctantly, dragging his feet, he took centre stage.

To the karaoke soundtrack, Mikhail sang a rousing, thigh-slapping, traditional Bulgarian folk song and we all applauded and laughed.

Then, with the garden night lights taking effect, offering a rainbow of hues, it was Alan's turn to sing. After placing his Rakia glass on the picnic table, he turned to Petar and asked, "Can I borrow your guitar?"

"Sure," Petar replied, handing the instrument

to Alan.

In tune and note perfect, Alan offered a sincere rendition of 'The First Time Ever I Saw Your Face' while gazing into my eyes. Of course, my heart melted and I hugged him, planting a long, smoochy, smouldering kiss on his lips. Maybe it was the love I felt for Alan or the effects of the Rakia, but the kiss did seem to linger for a long, long time.

After kicking off her shoes – I think the Rakia had something to do with that – Pavlina stepped on to the patio and belted out Mott the Hoople's 'Roll Away the Stone'. For some reason, Irena and yours truly became the backing singers, chanting "sha-la-la-la, push, push," while shoving imaginary boulders with our outstretched hands. By the third chorus, Irena had lost it and was laughing uncontrollably with tears of joy streaming down her face. We all demanded an encore and, eager to please, Pavlina took to the patio again.

Then it was my turn to sing. I stood on the patio and mumbled, "I can't sing." But by that juncture, they were all wrapped in their own amusement; they were too drunk to care. "Well," I muttered to myself, for no one was listening, "I did warn you..."

I sang, or rather squawked, 'Thank You for the Music'. Needless to say, I reduced my audience to tears of laughter, and someone – probably Alan –

uttered a mock boo. Well, in for a penny, in for a pound...I decided to go for it and, at the top of my voice, I truly murdered the song.

I took a bow and, polite to the end, my audience applauded, except for Irena, who was too busy wiping her eyes and holding her sides as she collapsed with mirth.

We sang and drank into the night. Then, with the moon high in the sky, Alan carried me into the bedroom where, well and truly chateaued, I rolled on to the pillow and slept.

Chapter Seven

Rakia, a word of caution – don't; it's potent stuff.

At some point in the morning, I crawled out of bed, my head in my hands for fear that it would roll off my shoulders.

I took a shower, standing under the cold water, my eyes wide and staring, like a catatonic zombie, then swallowed a handful of paracetamol, washed down with fruit juice. For this morning – and beyond that I didn't have a care – the pills and juice would serve as breakfast.

Alan and our hosts were up, all looking as fresh as daisies. Cheerfully they waved 'goodbye' as they set off for the university. I glimpsed Irena in the garden, tending her roses, then Mikhail as he wandered on to the patio from his room.

"Are you okay?" Mikhail asked while peering into my eyes, a solicitous frown creasing his forehead.

"A little hung-over," I confessed, "but I'm fine."

"Do you want to meet Ivan Simeonov?"

I opened my eyes in mild surprise. "He will talk with me?"

"I made a phone call, to his housekeeper, Maria Manova. I know Maria because I was friendly with Valya, her daughter. Maria is a widow. She is friendly. I think Ivan will talk with you."

"Great," I said, suddenly energised; "let's go."

I was still adjusting to the left-hand drive and with my senses scrambled by the Rakia, I thought it best to travel slowly. So we trundled along the road to Plovdiv, pausing around the halfway mark at the village of Mir.

I parked the car then studied my surroundings. I noted that some of the houses had grand facades and generous gardens, partially hidden behind graceful wrought-iron gates. However, the majority of the buildings were plain and basic. The village square consisted of a war memorial, a dried-out fountain and a sculpture depicting warriors harnessed to a plough. The main road was pot-holed while, to our left, chickens ran around in pens, scratching the dry ground. Straight ahead, three children stood on crusty concrete near a rusty roundabout in a bedraggled playground. The vehicles – a noisy bus, a dirty truck and several cars – would not have been out of place in a Humphrey Bogart movie, their longevity a testament to the communist workforce. Glancing round, the village struck me as homely, yet primitive, as though caught in a time warp.

On a street corner, I spied a pretty girl and a handsome boy. They stared at me, wary of a stranger.

"Romani," Mikhail explained.

"Do many Romani live here?"

He nodded. "There is a small community in Mir, and a larger community in the local prison."

"They cause trouble?" I asked cautiously.

"The Romani are a minority, and minorities are always the subject of racism, violence and propaganda. It is the same in your country?"

I nodded. "It is the same the world over. Some people must always oppress, whether in the name of communism or capitalism; some people must always feel superior."

We wandered past a number of farms and it occurred to me that the pace of life in Mir was slower than in the towns. As though to emphasise that point we paused to allow a horse and cart access to a driveway.

The farmhouses were built of stone and, clearly, were centuries old. Isolated, Ivan Simeonov's house was also built of stone. An attractive structure, patterned with large, irregular, coloured blocks, the house had a tiled roof forming a shallow V. Granite steps to the right of the building led to the first floor entrance while the garden path, overgrown with grass, consisted of large flagstones. The vineyard ran wild, its fruit neglected; furthermore, the rose bushes battled a thick bed of weeds.

Mikhail led me up the steps to the first floor

entrance. There, he knocked on a green door, its wood splintered with age, and we waited for Ivan Simeonov. However, it came as no surprise when his housekeeper, Maria Manova, opened the door.

As the door swung open, Maria studied me with cautious eyes while I appraised her. Pleasantly plump and five foot tall, she had dark hair, streaked with grey. Her eyes were attractive and the colour of chestnuts. Her face was lined with character and determination, carrying the burdens of late middle age. Indeed, her face betrayed a hint of melancholy. It was a face that belonged in the fields and meadows, bent over a hoe as its owner tilled the ground. I could picture Maria with the harvest on her shoulders and perspiration on her brow. Although a widow, she still wore her wedding ring, a simple gold band. Her earrings were gold studs while a gold crucifix sat upon her floral apron, prominent and proud.

"This is Maria Manova; she tends house for Ivan Simeonov. Maria, this is Samantha Smith from England."

"Wales," I corrected Mikhail.

"Sorry," he frowned. "Wales."

"Hello." I inclined my head and smiled at Maria.

"Hello Samantha from Wales; please, enter Ivan's house."

I stepped through the green door into a tall, square room furnished with dark oak fittings, bare floorboards and a naked electric light bulb. The walls were whitewashed and decorated with old and modern photographs, presumably Ivan's family spanning the generations. Ivan had reserved the far corner of the room for kitchen equipment: an ancient stove, copper pans and blue crockery, while a large armchair, its material threadbare, sat adjacent to a tall oak cupboard. From another room, presumably a bedroom, a clock ticked loudly, suggesting to me that Ivan was partially deaf. Clearly, the items in the living room had aged well beyond maturity, yet there was a sense of cleanliness about the place, a sense of order.

I glanced at a set of wooden chairs grouped around a square oak table. A handgun, a Soviet Makarov, rested on the table, on a cloth, its eight-round magazine disengaged.

Maria walked over to the weapon and inserted the magazine. Evidently, she'd been cleaning the gun and, her job complete, she returned it to the oak cupboard.

As Maria closed the cupboard door, I smiled and asked, "Do you know how to use that gun?"

She returned my smile, though the effort, apparently uncommon, appeared to strain her facial muscles. "We were taught in school, in communist times, so we could fight off the western aggressors."

Maria returned to the table. She folded the cloth neatly and placed it in a cupboard drawer. As she turned to face Mikhail, he asked, "How is Valya?"

Maria sighed then waved a hand in dismissive fashion. "Don't ask."

Mikhail offered an indifferent pout, shrugged, then continued, "Samantha is fascinated by our history. She would like to talk with Ivan about the war."

"I will call Ivan; he is resting, in his bedroom. Ivan has no English, but I will translate."

"You have excellent English," I said as Maria walked towards the bedroom.

She paused and gave her shoulders a gentle shrug. "From school, the TV, movies, books...I learn, a little."

My eyes wandered to a display cabinet containing silver trophies for boxing, fishing and hunting, along with a row of medals. I asked Maria about the medals. "Were they awarded to Ivan?"

"He was a brave soldier. He was decorated by the communists."

"He fought against the fascists."

She nodded. "Ivan was one of the leaders of Mir."

"And he managed to escape the slaughter."

Now she frowned, eyeing me with suspicion.

"You know about the slaughter?"

"Only a little," I confessed. "I know that the men of Mir were betrayed and that the fascists murdered them."

"Emil Angelov betrayed them," she said firmly. "To save his life, he sacrificed his comrades to the fascists. Of course, he lived in disgrace and was punished by the communists when they gained power." She hung her head sadly and gazed at the polished floorboards. "Emil's crime and the slaughter haunt our village to this day."

"Ivan lives in a fine house," I noted. "He prospered after the war?"

"He worked hard, as a gamekeeper. But the communists were grateful, they appreciated his commitment to the Resistance...they looked after their own."

Maria walked into the bedroom where she called Ivan Simeonov. Then with Maria's help, and a walking stick for support, the old man entered the living room and sat in his armchair.

Smartly dressed in a dark blue suit, akin to a 1930s mobster's suit, it was clear from his stooped walk and frail appearance that Ivan Simeonov was well into his nineties. Tall in his youth, age had withered him to a fragile question mark. He had a bald head, circled with a fine, white corona, neatly trimmed, blue rheumy eyes and a pugilist's face featuring a bent nose and scar tissue around his eyes. Clean-shaven, his face nevertheless contained patches of grey stubble, missed by the razorblade.

To Ivan, I smiled and said, "Thank you for meeting with me."

With Maria translating, Ivan replied, "It is a pleasure to have visitors."

"I would like to talk about the war; do you mind?"

As I spoke, Ivan cupped a hand behind his ear. He thought for a moment then leaned forward, resting his hands on his walking stick. After moistening his lips, he replied, "The war is in the past; I don't mind."

"It must have been a frightening time?"

He raised a wrinkled, liver-spotted hand and waved it airily, dismissing my comment. "We were too busy organising our lives, organising the Resistance; there was no time for fear."

"I bet you had some narrow escapes."

Now Ivan smiled. He stared at me while pointing at his head. "I had a bullet pass through my hat. Luckily, it was not flat on my head!"

I returned his smile then asked, "Were you in many gunfights?"

Now he scowled and growled, "If we had a chance to kill our enemy, we did."

"You are a brave man, Ivan Simeonov."

He shook his head, angrily, his face turning puce. While thumping his walking stick against the bare floorboards, he said, "Hristo Vazov, he was a brave man. Ivan Simeonov was only a soldier, following orders."

"Who is Hristo Vazov?"

"A fellow Resistance fighter. He had the heart of a lion and the courage of a tiger. He was a hero."

"Was he at the forest slaughter?"

Ivan shook his head. "No, he escaped."

"Is he still alive?"

Again, a shake of the weary head. "No longer. Hristo Vazov is dead."

"Were you at the slaughter?" I asked.

Ivan moistened his lips. With his walking stick between his legs, he leaned forward, his rheumy eyes staring at me with intent. "I had my gamekeeping duties to attend to; that night I was spared."

"You fought alongside Emil Angelov."

He nodded. "I knew Emil, yes."

"What was Emil like as a man?"

Ivan turned his head. While gazing at the wall he scowled. "Emil was a traitor, the worst of men."

"He betrayed your comrades?"

Distressed, Ivan glared at Maria and poured out a stream of vitriol. Frowning at me, Maria translated simply, "Ivan doesn't want to talk anymore."

"I understand," I said. "Thank you, Ivan, thank you for your time."

I followed Mikhail to the green door. There, I paused and glanced at Ivan. Clearly, he was upset and he shook violently as Maria helped him towards the bedroom. I'd stirred up some ghosts, that was for sure, and from the troubled look on Ivan's face, those ghosts were dancing through his head. That left me with an uneasy feeling; maybe the past was best left buried and I should concentrate on the present and the future instead.

Chapter Eight

We returned to the holiday home to find two of Mikhail's friends waiting for him. They'd arranged to travel into Plovdiv to play football so I advised him to go. Mikhail had played the role of travel guide to perfection and I had no wish to impinge on his time. Besides, I felt that he was becoming too fond of me, or maybe that was nothing more than my overactive imagination.

With a glass of iced fruit juice in my hand, I sat on the patio and watched as Irena tended her garden. My head was still sore after the Rakia and I was grateful for my sunglasses, to hide my bloodshot eyes.

Irena's garden was a riot of colour with poppies, sunflowers, yellow lilies, lavender and pink hydrangea in glorious bloom. She wandered between the walnut, apple, plum and peach trees, picking the fruit. Then she sterilized glass jars, in readiness for fruit preservation before cleaning a barrel, pungent with Petar's Rakia. Pausing, she drank bottled water from a hollowed out pumpkin, to cool her body and quench her thirst.

At one point, I felt guilty, sitting on a chaise longue while an eighty-six-year-old woman slaved under the hot afternoon sun. However, when I offered to help, Irena shooed me away insisting that she could manage on her own. So I retired to the house to gaze at Emil's picture.

As the daytime temperature climbed towards the forties, Irena, with perspiration dripping from her brow, decided to rest and entered the house. She saw me, looking at the photograph, and frowned. Then she offered an impish smile while her hands mimicked the action of driving a car.

"You want to ride with me in the car?" I asked, repeating her action.

"Da," Irena replied. "Yes."

"Where?" I asked. "Where shall we go?"

Irena pointed at the photograph, at her father.

"To Hisarya?"

She smiled, "Da."

"Okay," I threw my bag over my shoulder and led Irena to the car; "let's go."

Irena sat foursquare in the car, her elbows jutting out, her gaze proud as she stared through the windscreen. Dressed in a long black skirt and a black and white dappled blouse, she looked regal, yet humble, a queen in the best sense of that word.

A kilometre into our journey, Irena adjusted her wedding ring, which sat snug on her swollen fingers. Then she turned to gaze at me and started to sing. From her laughter, I had no doubt that she was recalling the karaoke.

"I have no singing voice," I replied defensively, my eyes scanning the rear-view mirror. "I did warn them..."

Irena continued to laugh. Then, from her handbag, she produced a picture of her father. "Emil..." She sang in graceful fashion and, while eyeing the road, I tried to make sense of her meaning.

"Emil, your father," I said, "he had a good voice, he loved singing?"

"Da," she shook her head, which I recalled meant a nod in western body language.

"He loved music?"

"Da." Irena raised her hands and mimicked the action of strumming a guitar.

"He played the guitar?"

"Da." Now she mimicked an artisan carving wood.

At first, I struggled to understand her meaning then it clicked, "The guitar Alan played last night...Emil made it for you?"

"Da." Irena's wrinkle-free face beamed with pride.

"It's a beautiful instrument; your father was a very talented man."

She wobbled her head and continued to smile, though I sensed that my words were lost on her.

At Hisarya, I parked the car. Then we walked

to the spring and the small stone shack. As we walked, Irena gathered a handful of wild flowers. She sniffed the bouquet then waved the flowers under my nose.

"Beautiful," I smiled.

She wobbled her head and replied, "Da."

We stood in silence for a moment, staring at the robbed out shack. Then Irena said, "Emil," and pointed at the flowers.

"He liked flowers, your father."

"Da." Gazing at the cloudless sky, she extended an arm and waved towards the heavens. Then she placed her hands to her head, to mimic sleep.

After a few false starts, I captured her meaning. "Emil studied the stars. He was an amateur astronomer."

"Da," Irena replied, pleased with me, pleased with herself.

"Before the war," I said, "it must have been a simpler time."

Irena frowned and I realised that my words were beyond her translation. Nevertheless, with a spring in her step, she walked towards the pure, clear water where she placed the flowers. Then she eased her hands together in quiet prayer. At that point I stood back, to allow Irena a private moment with her father. Later, I offered a helping hand, to guide her over the fallen masonry.

After climbing a grassy bank, I nodded towards the flowers and said, "Your father has no grave?"

Irena turned and stared into the forest. She waved an arm at the tall, fragrant pine trees, her eyes burdened, a heavy sadness troubling her face.

"The communists shot Emil in the forest and buried him there?"

"Da." Tears filled her eyes as she wobbled her head.

"Why did they do such a thing?" I asked, feeling Irena's sadness, her sense of indignation.

She raised a hand and drew a finger across her neck. "Predatel; traitor," she scowled, her face as black as thunder.

"Your father was a traitor?"

This time, Irena nodded her head, her way of saying, "no."

"Emil wasn't the traitor?"

Irena smiled. She grabbed my hands and squeezed my fingers, as though determined never to let go.

"Emil was innocent?"

Again, the smile and the firm grip on my fingers. Then I realised that she wanted me to hold on to that thought, that I was the one who should never let go.

"The communists shot the wrong man?"

In response, Irena wobbled her head.

"Who was the traitor?" I asked.

Irena pursed her lips together; she stared at the ground. As she glanced up, she offered an apologetic shrug.

"You don't know." To myself, I mused: I wonder if anyone knows.

We walked back to the car in silence, my mind preoccupied with Emil. I knew little about the man: he'd been a talented musician, a craftsman, an astronomer and a lover of nature. The image I had of him, gleaned through one sepia photograph, spoke of a gentle man, a man of peace moved to violence by the brutality of war. From Irena's reaction, I gauged that he'd loved her deeply and that she'd loved him. Indeed, it was patently clear that she still loved him. Could such a man betray his comrades? My instincts said 'no'.

We were travelling on the main road, back to Grozdovo, when I glanced in the rear-view mirror. Several glances later, I confirmed my suspicions. I pointed to the mirror and said, "We're being followed."

Cautiously, Irena looked over her shoulder. Her placid reaction reminded me that this was a woman who'd lived through wars, insurrections and periods of East-West paranoia; she would not overreact or scare easily. After smiling at me, she glanced down to her feet and indicated that I should lean on the accelerator.

"You think we should lose the tail?" I asked.

She wobbled her head and uttered a resounding, "Da."

First, I allowed the car, a gold Opel, to approach by driving slowly and by pausing at road junctions. I made a mental note of the number plate, a combination of two letters, four numbers and two more letters, then I hit the gas and allowed the wheels to kick up dust.

As we sped along the open road, the Opel accelerated. The driver, male, was young and apparently fearless. Furthermore, he had local knowledge to aid his pursuit. However, I am nothing if not resourceful and I noticed a forest track, which horse-shoed away from, then back on to, the main road. The track ran for about three kilometres, an ideal distance for my purpose.

Turning sharply to my left, I entered the forest. The plume of dust in my rear-view mirror told me that the Opel was in pursuit. Relying on the fact that my Suzuki was smaller and better suited to the narrow dirt track than the cumbersome Opel, I put my foot down and completed a dusty lap. Back on the main road I turned towards Hisarya, not Grozdovo, then entered the forest again. Although some distance back the Opel was still tailing us. However, by the third lap he was no longer in view.

On completing the third lap, I turned towards Grozdovo. Unable to see us, the Opel would follow our pattern and turn towards Hisarya then enter the forest again; at least, that was my plan. By the time he'd realised his mistake, we'd be long gone.

After studying the rear-view mirror for another kilometre I judged that we'd been successful. For the moment at least, we'd lost our tail.

Turning to Irena, I smiled and she grinned with satisfaction. With her elbows jutting out, she stared through the windscreen, her melodic voice offering the proud cry, "Bravo, Samantha; bravo!"

Chapter Nine

Back at the mountain home, the carnivores enjoyed an evening meal of kapama – a range of meats covered with rice, peppers and pickled cabbage, topped with a large sausage and baked in clay pots – while I munched my way through another salad.

"I thought Dr Tresillian spoke well today," Pavlina said, pausing between mouthfuls of kapama, "about social control, rehabilitation and behavioural techniques."

Alan nodded. He dabbed his lips with a napkin, sampled his wine then said, "She made several good points, and I tend to agree with her. It is possible to change behaviour patterns through aversion therapy, cognitive therapy, modelling, etc, but the major problem is most penal systems are unscientific: assumptions are made without proper testing and monitoring. The huge re-offending rates prove that 'punishment' does not work, but there is little attempt to alter the system. Court judgements and convictions are usually based on personal and out-dated legal opinion, public pressure, social isolation, revenge and tradition. Social rehabilitation is tagged on at the end, if it's tagged on at all."

Pavlina inclined her head in agreement while stirring her kapama with a silver fork. Then she turned to a recalcitrant Mikhail and said, "Come on, Misho, eat your dinner."

"I'm not hungry," Mikhail complained. Abruptly, he rose from the table and walked towards his room. "I need a lie down."

"Is he unwell?" Alan asked.

"He's love sick," Petar mumbled while helping himself to an additional sausage.

"He's fallen for Samantha?" Pavlina gasped, her eyes wide, staring at each of us in turn, before settling on me.

"I'm sorry," I spluttered apologetically, my words tangling with a mouthful of lettuce, "I didn't lead him on, I promise."

"Don't worry about it," Petar said calmly. He splashed some wine into my glass before adding a generous measure to his own. "It is not your fault. Mikhail is at an impressionable age. To him, this is a holiday romance, an intense, passionate affair; he will get over it."

Pavlina paused, a forkful of kapama poised before her ruby lips. She considered her husband's words then ate, slowly, thoughtfully.

Later, as Petar served the sweet – torta, a delicious cake – Pavlina said, "My mother tells me that you went for a ride to Hisarya."

I nodded. "I've enjoyed another interesting day. First, I called on Ivan Simeonov and talked with him. He was open at the beginning then became reticent. After Mir and Ivan's house, we went to Hisarya. On the way back, we were followed."

"Followed?" Petar raised an eyebrow, his interest piqued. "By whom?"

"I don't know. The car was a gold Opel," I informed my hosts before reeling off the registration number.

"It means nothing to me," Petar added with a frown.

"Nor me," Pavlina said, her thin face concerned, anxious.

"Why would anyone follow you?" Petar asked, his posture languid as he leaned back in his chair, sipping his wine.

"Irena thinks that her father was innocent; he didn't betray his comrades."

On hearing my words, Pavlina sighed. She turned to her mother and scowled. "It is a daughter's wish. At some point in every year Irena states that Emil was innocent and she gives voice to that dream; but everyone knows the facts."

"What are the facts?" I asked while leaning forward, placing my elbows on the table. "The communist Resistance fighters, our allies, were betrayed and massacred in the forest near Mir. Emil and Ivan Simeonov escaped the massacre, by one means or another. The fascists, the murderers, spared Emil and announced that he was the traitor. There is no other evidence against Emil."

We sat in thoughtful silence, mulling over my words. Throughout our tête-à-tête Irena had eyed me intently, the force of her presence urging me on. Although our words had flown thick and fast, too fast for Irena to understand them, she sensed the nature of our conversation, felt the friction around the table, the air of unease.

"But," Pavlina protested, "the communists questioned Emil when they seized power; they were convinced that he was the traitor."

"But were witnesses called?" I asked. "Was evidence taken? As I understand it, the communists conducted this 'trial' during the heat of war when emotions were raw and people were looking for a scapegoat. By that time, the people of Mir were convinced that Emil was the traitor and their word went against him. His protests of innocence, even if he did protest, would have carried little weight."

"All this took place seventy years ago," Pavlina complained; "we will never learn the truth."

Petar leaned forward. He licked the middle finger of his right hand then gathered together the crumbs of torta, lifting them from his plate. While sucking his finger, he said to his wife, "You might be right, sweetie, but someone disagrees with your statement."

"The person who followed Sam today," Alan said heavily, his mind no doubt recalling past events, my previous 'misadventures'.

"Are you sure that you were followed?" Pavlina asked earnestly. She'd consumed her kapama, but her torta and wine, she'd barely touched.

"I've tailed and been tailed often enough to know when I'm being followed."

"Word of your interest in Emil must have reached your pursuers very quickly," Petar surmised while nibbling a sliver of goats' cheese.

I nodded. Word had reached our pursuers very quickly indeed. While mulling over that point, I said, "At a guess, they heard soon after I'd talked with Ivan Simeonov."

"What will you do now?" Petar asked.

"I'll talk with Ivan again. That is, if Irena and Pavlina are willing."

Pavlina turned to Irena and the two women talked earnestly in Bulgarian. From their tone and body language, I sensed that Pavlina was wary while Irena was keen that I should meet with Ivan.

Eventually, the conversation cooled and with a sense of harmony restored, Pavlina nodded and said, "It is our wish that you should talk with Ivan. We must learn the truth."

"Da," Irena added forcefully, the matriarch

asserting her will.

In bed that night, I reflected that Irena was telling the truth, that her words were not coloured by emotion and a desire to re-write the past. Also, my questions had disturbed someone – the real traitor? Someone with a need or desire to keep the secret, buried in the past? Ivan's reaction told me that walking with ghosts can be painful and I was reluctant to trample over too many souls. However, Irena deserved the truth; in the winter of her days, she required an answer; for her I would follow in Emil's footsteps and seek to unveil the secrets of the past.

Chapter Ten

The following morning I sat on the patio, sunhat on my head, sunglasses perched on my nose, gazing at the Rhodope Mountains, at a white monument dedicated to war heroes. I wondered about Emil Angelov – a hero to Irena, a traitor to others – and the sins of fathers in general, including the misdeeds of my own, wayward, dad.

A mosquito nipped my upper arm, dragging my thoughts back to the present. And with my mind on home, I tried to connect with Faye.

"How are things at the office?" I asked as Faye flickered into life on my mobile phone.

"Fine."

"How's Marlowe?"

"See for yourself." Faye angled the computer and the cat came into view. He was licking his paws and washing his ears. His left ear was split, I noticed, no doubt due to a cat fight. Ah, the rough and tumble life of an alley cat, and the secrets he kept.

"Any luck with finding a permanent job?" I asked and Faye angled the computer again, admiring herself as she came into view. As a teenager, Faye had dreamt of becoming a model and the vanity of that profession betrayed itself sometimes, especially in unguarded moments.

"Nah," she sighed, "no luck with the jobs. I went for an interview yesterday, but I fracked it up."

"How?" I asked.

"They asked me about the blank spell on my CV." In embarrassment, she looked away, offering her profile. With her mind agitated, her fingers busied themselves, tidying my desk. "What could I tell them?" she moaned. "The truth? That I'd been a hooker. I tried to lie and made a fracking mess of it. No one wants me, Sam; no one wants a hooker."

"Ex-hooker," I corrected Faye.

She stood and walked out of shot. With her voice harsh, she talked into thin air. "You can never shake off your past, Sam; to some people, I'll always be a whore."

"You're not a whore, Faye; there were reasons why you did what you did."

"Yeah, maybe; but apart from you, who's gonna care; who's gonna take the time to understand and listen?"

We waited, for Faye to compose herself, for her mood to brighten, for her pretty face to come into view. Then she asked, "How are things with you?"

"I'm looking into the past." I explained about my talk with Ivan Simeonov and my trip to Hisarya.

"Sounds interesting," Faye said, her eyes

wandering to the desk, to the neatly squared papers and files, then to her red fingernails. "Mind you don't walk on any toes. If you frack things up you'll be looking at a spell in a Bulgarian prison."

"No thank you to that," I said hastily. "I'll be careful where I tread."

"Oh, I nearly forgot," Faye added as an afterthought. "Mr Fry called; he'd like you to deliver a bankruptcy notice."

"Can't it wait until I get back?"

"Urgent, Mr Fry said." Faye gazed at the camera, her face vacant, as though staring into a void. Then her features brightened and I could almost see the cogs clicking as she came up with an idea. "I tell you what; I'll deliver it for you."

I felt a shiver of anxiety, despite the oppressive heat. "Fry, Gouldman and Fletcher are important clients, Faye, don't screw up."

"I'm only delivering a letter, how can I screw that up?"

"Okay," I conceded. "But don't screw up."

Faye grinned, revealing her even, perfect, milky-white teeth. "Speak again soon," she said. And I was left to reflect that if the Devil did walk on Earth, she'd disguise herself as an angel, and that maybe she was already in my office, sitting at my desk.

To add to my sense of unease, Mikhail

wandered on to the patio. He eyed me for a moment, kicked a football around then disappeared into his room.

I checked my watch: time was ticking, approaching noon, time to travel to Ivan's cottage. And with Mikhail in this mood, it was best to travel alone.

I drove to Mir, to Ivan's cottage, parked the car then skipped up the granite steps. At the green door, I paused, knocked and called Ivan's name. No answer. So I called Maria's name, only to receive no reply. I knocked again and discovered that the door was ajar. After adjusting my shoulder bag, I eased the door open and stepped inside.

The heat from the room and the loud ticking of the clock hit me. Then the sight of broken glass assaulted my senses: someone had raided Ivan's trophy cabinet; his medals were missing. I tiptoed over to the cabinet, mindful that this was a crime scene, ensuring that I did not disturb any evidence. The trophies were still there, but the medals were definitely missing. After confirming that fact, I glanced around, studying the rest of the room.

As previously, the room appeared neat, with nothing untoward or out of place. The crime had been a clean one, which raised my suspicions. Either the thief knew exactly what he was about, or it was an 'inside job'.

Turning away from the cabinet, I walked towards the bedroom. As with the green door, the bedroom door was ajar. Using my elbow, to avoid leaving any fingerprints, I nudged the door open and entered the room.

Inside the bedroom, the ticking from the clock reached industrial levels; indeed, the noise emanating from the brass timepiece was enough to wake the dead. A small plaque on the clock suggested that it had been presented to Ivan in recognition of dutiful service.

With the clock clanging in my ears, I approached a brass-framed bed. Dressed in his mobster's suit, Ivan lay on the bed, his eyes wide and staring, his mouth agape. I'd been wrong about the clock: despite its clanging, it would not wake the dead. A nonagenarian, had Ivan died of natural causes? Or had he disturbed the burglar?

I dipped my fingers into my shoulder bag and reached for my phone. Then I wracked my brain for the Bulgarian emergency number; something at the back of my mind told me that the number was 112. I was about to dial that number when I heard footsteps in the living room, walking across the polished floorboards. Before I could react, a hand pushed the bedroom door open and Maria Manova stepped into the room. She glanced at me, at Ivan, then opened her mouth to scream. Her shrieks alerted a passerby and soon he was with us, his eyes wide as he scanned the room. To Maria, I tried to explain in slow, careful English, but the sight of Ivan had provoked a fit of hysterics and I couldn't get through. The man, a forty-something farmer with a rosy complexion and round shoulders, eyed me with suspicion, and a sense of accusation. He uttered something in Bulgarian and even I realised that he was yelling for the cops.

Chapter Eleven

Led by Detective Vasil Petrov, the Bulgarian police secured the crime scene. While forensic scientists searched for evidence, Maria and the farmer offered their statements, and the detective sat with me in Ivan's overgrown garden beside a weather-beaten table.

"A man is dead," Petrov said, unbuttoning his shirt and loosening his tie; he wore a white shirt, short-sleeved, petrol blue trousers and a matching tie. "You are a friend of my friends, but I must conduct a formal interview."

"I understand," I said.

"But, before the formalities, maybe we could talk..."

I nodded then removed my sunglasses so that Detective Petrov could look into my eyes and see that I had nothing to hide.

"You entered Ivan Simeonov's cottage?"

"Yes."

"Uninvited?"

"I knocked on the door, I called his name...I sensed that something was amiss."

"The door was unlocked?"

"Yes."

"Did you see anyone in the house, in the

garden?"

"No one," I replied.

Detective Petrov adjusted his tie. He twisted his neck, as though to relieve a knot of tension. While massaging the back of his neck, he asked, "Why did you call on Ivan Simeonov?"

"To talk with him about the war."

"You have an interest in the war?"

"I have an interest in the Hermit of Hisarya."

"Emil Angelov," Detective Petrov mused, his hand wandering from his neck to the stubble on his chin. "The traitor."

I shrugged, "So legend states."

Petrov leaned forward. He stared at me with intent, through narrow eyes. "You think Emil Angelov was innocent?"

"What do you think?" I asked, keen to hear the detective's opinion.

Petrov sat back. He turned his head, offering his powerful, leonine profile. In weary tones, he said, "I have not given the matter much thought."

"Everyone assumes that Emil was guilty."

Petrov nodded. "That seems a fair assumption. The community blame Emil for the betrayal and my friends, Pavlina and Irena, carry that weight to this day. But," he added, leaning forward, nodding towards his fellow officers as they searched the garden for evidence, "let us return to Ivan

Simeonov; maybe he died of natural causes; after all, he was in his nineties."

"But you suspect foul play."

Detective Petrov's lips twitched into a painful smile. "Ivan's trophy cabinet was broken into; his medals have gone."

"Are burglaries common in Mir?" I asked.

"All the valuable land and the valuables are owned by farmers and the farmers carry shotguns..."

I nodded. It was an elegant answer, and a colourful way to say 'no'.

We paused while a junior officer talked with Detective Petrov in Bulgarian. The detective nodded and grunted, sighed and groaned. Then he dismissed his subordinate, who returned to Ivan's house to continue his investigations.

"We would like to search your car," Petrov said; "do you have any objections?"

"None whatsoever...feel free...be my guest."

"We will take the car, and yourself, into Plovdiv...for your return, shall I arrange alternative transport?"

"I will phone Alan or Petar," I said, "assuming that word hasn't already reached them."

Petrov placed his elbows on the gnarled old table. While his fingers formed a bridge, he stared at the knots in the wood. He placed his chin on his fingers then gazed at me; he studied me, assessed me, as though through silence he could determine the truth.

Whatever his conclusions, Detective Petrov kept them to himself and in silence we sat, until a colleague interrupted us again. This time a female officer spoke with Petrov and although I couldn't be sure, I think the discussion centred on Maria Manova.

"Did Ivan Simeonov have any enemies?" I asked as the female detective returned to her duties and wandered out of earshot.

"Not that I know of," Petrov replied in his customary low grumble. "Ivan lived a quiet, peaceable life in retirement."

A bee buzzed around my head, possibly mistaking the sweat on my brow for nectar. I brushed it away with my sunhat then said, "I was followed yesterday, after I'd talked with Ivan, by a man driving a gold Opel Kadett." I informed Detective Petrov of the registration number.

Petrov delved into his trouser pocket. He produced a pen and a notebook and made a note of the registration number. "I will check this out," he said while tapping his notebook with a thick index finger. He adjusted his wedding band, a ring of white gold, then asked, "Do you have any idea why you were followed?"

"I can only think that there's a connection to my questions about Emil Angelov."

"Maybe you would be wise not to ask any more questions about Emil," Petrov said sagely. "Take my advice: after you have delivered your formal statement, return to your hosts; enjoy their hospitality and our country; enjoy your holiday; leave the past to the past and leave the death of Ivan Simeonov to the police."

Chapter Twelve

At a police station in Plovdiv, I offered my formal statement to a female officer, the officer who'd talked with Detective Petrov at Ivan's house. Then Petar arrived to transport me to his home.

We were sitting around the dinner table, in silence, though Mikhail was absent, mooching in his room. From the quiet, subdued atmosphere, I sensed that I was not flavour of the month, so I made my excuses and left.

I knocked on Mikhail's door and he said, "Enter." Easing the door open, I stepped into the room.

It was clear that Mikhail's room belonged to a teenager: he'd draped his clothes over a radiator while other items littered the floor; books and CDs cluttered a desk while posters adorned the walls.

"Nice room," I said, my smile bright and diplomatic.

"It's okay," Mikhail shrugged, rolling off his bed.

"You support Chelsea," I noted, eyeing a football poster.

"Yeah." While standing beside me, he turned and gazed at the poster, a team photograph of smiling, sporting millionaires.

"Not Lokomotiv Plovdiv," I chided.

Mikhail frowned. He said solemnly, "Lokomotiv Plovdiv will never win the Champions League."

I glanced around the room, buying time, searching for a way in, for a way to broach the awkward subject of unrequited love. Eventually, I thought of a solution and said, "I'm sorry if I've upset you."

"You haven't upset me," Mikhail mumbled, turning, offering his shoulder, his eyes wandering over his desk.

"Come and join us at the dinner table," I urged.

"I'm not hungry," he said, shaking his head.

I sighed, thought for a moment then continued, "When I was your age, I met this man. Actually, I never met him; I just saw him and became infatuated. He never even realised that I was there or knew of my existence. I thought this man was gorgeous, the man of my dreams. I convinced myself that I was deeply, passionately in love with him, that I would wait for him forever, that I would want no other and love no one else. Then, one day, I saw him walking hand in hand with another woman. I felt betrayed. Upset, I vowed to have nothing to do with men. Of course, time moved on and my feelings changed. In fact, I can hardly recall that man now; I have no memory of his looks or what attracted me to him in the first place." I shuffled my feet, altered my position and stood in front of Mikhail. "What I'm trying to say is, I'm just a moment in your life; there will be other moments and those moments will be more meaningful."

He sighed, stared at the ceiling then averted his gaze. In a strangled voice, he said, "You are more than a moment in my life. You are in my heart, forever."

"No, Mikhail."

He turned and dramatically dropped to one knee. Taking my hands in his, he said, "Samantha, I love you."

"But...," I complained.

"You cannot say but," Mikhail insisted. "I love you with all my passion." He stood and pulled me close, gripping my arms. "Your boyfriend is too old for you; you are young, full of life, vitality, you need someone like me, someone to share your passion."

I pulled away, turned my back and said, "Alan and I share a very passionate love life."

"You say that to shock me," Mikhail shouted, his tone betraying his anger.

I stared at my sandals, aware that the conversation was not going as planned.

"You do not shock me," Mikhail insisted. "And I forgive you. But from now, I want you to be the love of my life."

Although it was alien to me, I realised that I should assert myself. Drawing myself up to my modest five foot five, I turned to face Mikhail and said, "It's not possible."

"Make it possible, Samantha," Mikhail pleaded. "For my sanity, for my soul, you must make it possible."

I was thinking of an exit line when we heard voices in the corridor. Someone had called at Petar's house and from the low grumble and morose tone, I guessed that that someone was Detective Vasil Petrov.

Mikhail placed a finger to his lips and an ear to the door. He listened intently as Petar and Petrov talked in Bulgarian, Pavlina adding the occasional, high-pitched word.

"Ivan was murdered," Mikhail translated in a conspiratorial whisper, "it is confirmed; he was suffocated." After listening at the door again, Mikhail's jaw dropped; he turned to me and said, "Witnesses say that you did it."

"Witnesses?" I frowned. "But, I never touched Ivan. They must be mistaken..."

Mikhail shook his head in decisive fashion. "No; no mistake; Detective Petrov is here to arrest you."

Befuddled and confused, I searched my mind for a reply.

In the depths of my confusion, Mikhail grabbed my hand and dragged me towards the window. "Quick," he insisted, assisting me over the window ledge. "We must run; we must escape..."

Chapter Thirteen

We ran into the forest, stumbling in our desperation, following a stream, its banks strewn with large stones and boulders. Although night was closing in, light filtered through the dense forest, offering a pale green glow as it kissed the leaves. The stream cascaded over a waterfall, maybe four metres high, its spray soaking my skin while water tumbled through the fissures in the rock face, splashing into a turquoise pool. Vegetation surrounded the pool along with a number of rocks, green with a luxuriant covering of moss.

"You will be safe here," Mikhail insisted as we entered a cave rich with stalactites and stalagmites. "We can shelter here. I will catch fish from the river and cook it for breakfast."

"I'm a vegetarian," I sighed, aware that Mikhail had overlooked that rather blatant fact. "You don't know my tastes and habits, Mikhail, you don't know me. You're not in love with me; you're in love with the idea of being in love."

Mikhail frowned. He turned away, ostensibly to study a line of modern graffiti, scratched into the rock. From the dawn of time people, caves and drawings have been linked through artistic expression; it's as though underground caverns are natural galleries.

"You talk strange at times," Mikhail complained; "I do not understand you."

On another occasion, it would have been a pleasure to visit the caves, but with darkness all around and the evening chill touching my bare shoulders, I felt a sense of disquiet and unease.

Animated and excited, with the adrenaline flowing following our scramble through the forest, Mikhail grabbed my hand and led me deeper into the cave. While admiring a large stalactite, beautifully wrought by nature, he said, "Tradition states that people were married in these caves."

After an involuntary shiver, due to the evening chill and my predicament, I freed my hand from Mikhail's grip and turned to walk towards the entrance. "I'm not sure this is wise. I think we've made a mistake." With pleading eyes, I turned to face Mikhail. "I think we should return to your parents."

"But...," Mikhail spluttered, "Detective Petrov will arrest you. You will spend twenty years in a Bulgarian gaol."

I stood at the entrance to the cave, gazing at the turquoise pool and the cascading water. Somewhere in the darkness, in the forest, a creature stirred and scurried into the undergrowth. A twig snapped, an owl hooted; the trees offered a sense of movement, as though they were listening to you, closing in.

While sitting on a boulder, beside the pool, I said, "I will explain to Detective Petrov that the witnesses are mistaken; I did not murder Ivan Simeonov."

"But the witnesses are adamant," Mikhail said, splashing a pebble into the pool, "they saw you murder the old man."

"Who are the witnesses?" I asked my eyes on the ripples as they floated towards the water's edge.

"Detective Petrov named Maria Manova and Natasha Stefanova."

I drew my knees up, placed my hands on my knees and my chin on my hands. I sat in that contemplative position, on the boulder, like an over-grown pixie or elf. "Why would Maria say such a thing?" I asked. "It's as evident as the hills around Plovdiv that she's lying."

"Maria is an honest person," Mikhail insisted; "she does not lie. If Maria says you murdered Ivan Simeonov, people will believe her."

"Why would she lie?"

Mikhail shrugged. "I can think of no reason."

Neither could I, but there had to be a reason. Theft? Did Maria Manova steal Ivan Simeonov's medals? The theft would offer a motive. On balance, Maria struck me as an honest person, yet something had compelled her to lie.

Turning to face Mikhail, I asked, "Who is the other witness, Natasha...?"

"Stefanova. I do not know this name or this woman, but she swears also that you murdered Ivan Simeonov." Mikhail joined me beside the boulder. He stared at me through troubled eyes. "Tell me, honestly, Samantha; did you kill the old man?" Hastily, he added, "I will still love you, even if you are a murderer."

"I did not kill Ivan," I replied wearily, disturbed by his question, his train of thought. If a person who claimed passionate love for you could hold such doubts, where did that place the non-committed, like Detective Petrov?

"I believe you," Mikhail said. He placed a hand on my shoulder then echoed my thoughts, "But many, including the police, will have their doubts."

I slipped off the boulder and stood beside the pool. The moon was high in the sky now and reflected on the water. It occurred to me that searching for the truth was akin to casting your net, fishing for the moon; it was a thankless task with the odds stacked against you. However, I had no option; I had to cast my net and fish for the truth.

"We must return," I insisted. "Any more of this and you'll be in trouble."

"Samantha...," Mikhail hesitated. He stood before me, a youth on the verge of manhood. With the moon highlighting his face, knighting his shoulders, casting long shadows, he said solemnly, "You doubt my love for you, I can see. You think I am childish and immature, a boy. We will return, and when we return I will show you what love means; I will show you the depth of my love."

Chapter Fourteen

In the early hours of the morning, we returned to the mountain home to find the lights on, burning through the darkness, offering a threatening, not welcoming, glare.

"Samantha...Mikhail." As we entered the living room, Pavlina jumped up from her position, perched on the edge of an armchair. Irena sat in her rocking chair, looking concerned, running her fingers over a rosary, while Petar stood at his wife's side, an air of resigned patience etched on his face. Alan was also in the room, sitting on the sofa. His left eyebrow twitched, offering a modicum of emotion; otherwise, his face remained impassive, impossible to read.

"Where have you been, Mikhail?" With her initial relief subsiding, Pavlina frowned, betraying her anger.

"It's my fault, not Mikhail's," I said, stepping into the room. "We overheard Detective Petrov talking about Ivan's murder, panicked and ran. I'm to blame, not Mikhail." I paused and watched as the strain visibly dropped from Pavlina's face. As though to say, "don't worry", Petar placed an arm around his wife's shoulders and gave her a hug. "Please, telephone Detective Petrov," I continued; "I will explain my actions to him."

Petar glanced at Alan and the two men nodded. Then Petar fished his phone from his trouser pocket and called the police. While we waited for Detective Petrov, Pavlina said, "Mikhail, go to your room; we will talk later."

I offered Mikhail a rueful glance then said, "I apologise for everything; I didn't mean to bring trouble to your door."

Irena said something in Bulgarian, and the family gathered round the matriarch to listen. Meanwhile, Alan took advantage of the distraction to guide me to our bedroom.

"Care to explain," he said while leaning against the door.

"I panicked. The thought of spending twenty years in a Bulgarian gaol, away from you, away from everything I hold dear, made me run."

Alan nodded. Maybe he was angry, maybe he was furious, but his face betrayed no emotion while his even tone revealed that he was in control. He gave the fine hairs on his chin a thoughtful rub and said, "People who run invariably look guilty."

"I know," I sighed, flopping on to the bed. "I'm in a hole."

"And how will you climb out?" Alan asked, his forehead furrowing, suggesting that he was lost for an answer.

"By telling the truth."

"It's your word against two witnesses," he pointed out.

"The witnesses are lying."

"Obviously," Alan nodded, entertaining no doubt. "Any idea why?"

I shook my head then ran my fingers through my hair, combing through my exasperation. "No."

"Petar tells me that Maria is regarded as a pillar of the community. She is industrious, honest and well-liked."

"And Natasha Stefanova?"

"Natasha owns a beauty salon in the city; Petar knows nothing about her, apart from that."

We paused to gather our thoughts, to consider a possible solution. At home I could rely on Detective Inspector 'Sweets' MacArthur and a small network of reliable contacts to bail me out of trouble, but here I could rely on no one, apart from Alan and my wits.

"There's a chance that Petrov will arrest you," Alan said, "that you'll spend some time in gaol."

"I know." I tugged my hair and thumped the mattress in frustration. Despite my best efforts, I could not think clearly; a way forward would not present itself.

"This could drag on for months," Alan sighed.

I nodded. Months, even years. I groaned, "It

will mean the end of my agency."

Alan walked over to the bed. He pulled me to my feet and gave me a hug. He knew how much my agency meant to me; I fervently hoped that he knew how much he meant to me. Dressed in a tee-shirt and shorts, as ever, he looked handsome, debonair, and I was grateful for his strong, bronzed arms, grateful for his support. Looking on the bright side, a crisis like this might draw us even closer together; or it could force us apart.

"I'll talk with the people at the Embassy," Alan said after kissing my forehead. "I'll arrange legal support."

I gave him a hug then placed my head against his chest. "I'm a trouble magnet, aren't I?"

He chuckled, quietly, to himself. "You can say that again."

"As Faye would say, I've fracked it up."

Alan kissed my forehead again. He stroked my hair. "You've placed your dainty feet on some big toes, to say the least."

"Whose toes?" I asked, pulling away, staring through the window, into the darkness, into the void, as though searching for an answer. "Who would want Ivan dead?"

Alan paused. He thought for a moment then said, "Someone connected to the Second World War massacre..."

"But with Ivan gone," I reasoned, "they're all dead."

"...someone who knows the truth about the massacre and is determined to keep it a secret."

"For what reason?" I shrugged. "We're talking about something that happened seventy years ago."

"Yes," Alan smiled. He raised his index finger, a typical reaction when making a sage point. "But look at Irena, at the people you've talked with; the massacre is a large part of Mir's psyche; the village lost most of its men that day; you should not underestimate the power of the past, especially when the past is relived through collective memory."

As I absorbed that point, Petar rapped on the bedroom door. "Sorry to interrupt, but Detective Petrov has arrived."

Alan opened the door. We glanced at each other then followed Petar into the living room. There, we found Detective Petrov, looking as lugubrious as ever, and somewhat tired. You might say he was carrying the world on his shoulder, but that would have made him an unbalanced man. I think it's fairer to say that he was carrying the world and its doppelganger on his shoulders, and that the weight was weighing him down.

"We have found Ivan's medals," he announced morosely, "in a small sack, in your car." He shrugged then bowed towards me. "I am sorry, I must arrest you."

"The medals were planted," I said, "but I understand."

We were about to walk out of the house, towards Petrov's car, when Mikhail appeared, his face flushed, his expression anxious. Pushing past his father, he stood before the detective and said, "No; Samantha is innocent."

"Not now, Mikhail." Pavlina brushed him away, as though sweeping aside a mosquito; "go to your room; we will talk later."

"But Samantha is innocent," Mikhail protested.

Pavlina placed her hands on her hips. She was about to raise her voice again, and from the scowl on her face vent her anger, when Detective Petrov stepped forward, a curious frown creasing his brow.

"Let the boy speak," Petrov insisted. "You can provide the lady with an alibi?"

"No," Mikhail shook his head.

"Then how do you know that she is innocent?"

Mikhail glanced at his mother, at his father; he stared at Alan, at me; then his gaze fell on Vasil Petrov. "I know," Mikhail announced, his head held high, his face solemn, his voice firm and proud, "because I, Mikhail Dimitrov, murdered Ivan Simeonov." He thrust his hands forward, inviting the cold steel of handcuffs. "Arrest me, Detective

Petrov; I am the murderer."

Chapter Fifteen

I travelled in a blue and white police car, into the centre of Plovdiv. There, Detective Petrov invited me into the police station, a building of steel and smoked glass.

Under the harsh strip lights, and to the syncopated soundtrack of slamming doors and echoing feet we walked along a long corridor, a corridor that reeked of floor polish and fresh paint, into a small interview room. The interview room had a high ceiling, a noisy radiator, a desk riddled with woodworm and a small, creaky chair. The stench of stale cigarettes and shoe polish assaulted my nostrils, along with the strongest stench of all, the smell of fear.

"Do you want legal representation?" Detective Petrov asked, drawing a second chair away from the table before sitting opposite me.

"At this stage, no."

"Then we will talk 'off the record'."

I nodded. "I'm happy with that."

Detective Petrov was cutting me a fair amount of slack; I was aware of that. Maybe he was hoping that I'd trip myself up, then offer a confession, or maybe he empathised with my plight and was repaying a favour to his friends, Pavlina and Petar.

Mikhail had travelled in a separate police car, to a different police station where, I guessed, the police were interviewing him.

"Did you murder Ivan Simeonov?" Petrov asked, his voice heavy, his brow furrowed, his swarthy features set with determination and a fierce resolve.

"No, I did not."

"But you did take an interest in his medals."

I nodded, pursed my lips, then asked, "And that's my motive for murder, theft?"

"It is." Petrov inclined his head, bowing slightly.

"I admired Ivan's medals out of courtesy," I explained. "I do not believe in medals; a trinket does not make one man braver than another; many heroes are lost or unrecorded by history."

Petrov leaned back. He placed his left hand on the desk and quietly drummed his fingers. His fingernails were short and neatly manicured while a small bruise troubled his ring finger, possibly the result of a DIY mishap.

"I tend to agree," he said, his voice a cross between a groan and a grumble, "a medal is not necessarily a mark of courage; but some people will pay good money to acquire such awards."

Leaning forward, I asked, "Who said that I eyed Ivan's medals?"

"Maria Manova."

"And in that, she speaks the truth."

"But of the murder she speaks a lie?" Petrov asked, lifting his left hand from the desk, caressing the thick mane at the back of his head.

"I like Maria, I believe the good things I've heard about her; but in regard to the murder, she speaks a lie."

Petrov strained his neck muscles, leaning against his left hand, circling his head. Pausing at the end of his calisthenics, he stared into my eyes and growled, "Why would she lie?"

"To protect the murderer."

"Mikhail Dimitrov?"

In spite of myself, I smiled, "You know as well as I that Mikhail is no murderer."

"Then why the confession?" Petrov asked reasonably.

"Mikhail regards his confession as a noble gesture, a demonstration of his love for me."

Detective Petrov puffed out his cheeks. His left hand tapped his shirt pocket, above his left breast. It was the action of a man searching for cigarettes. I guessed that at some point in his past, Vasil Petrov had been a smoker and from the tense look on his face, I sensed that he was ready to take up the weed again.

"Do you love Mikhail Dimitrov?" Petrov asked

while leaning forward, placing his hands together, resting his elbows on the desk. For some reason, I pictured us playing an intellectual game of chess, repositioning our pieces, seeking an advantage, looking for a move that would lead to checkmate.

"I'm in love with my fiancé, Dr Alan Storey," I replied truthfully.

"And the boy, Mikhail, has fallen for your charms?"

I nodded, my eyes fixed on the desk. "Sadly, yes."

Petrov sighed. He stood then circled the desk, his tread heavy, his gaze thoughtful, his hands clasped behind his back like a member of the British royal family. After completing four circuits, he said, "I am tempted to castigate Mikhail as a fool but, as I am a man too, and you are blessed with a number of, er...," he paused to run an appreciative eye over my feminine features, "charms, I can understand his romantic gesture." Petrov puckered his lips and threatened to smile. "Tell me, do you get into trouble like this at home?"

"Sometimes," I confessed.

"And your fiancé tolerates your troubles?"

I nodded and reflected, "Alan is a very tolerant man."

Petrov offered a sage expression then paused as a colleague entered the room. He accepted a file from his colleague, a thickset man with a ruby birthmark adorning his forehead. He talked with the man in whispered Bulgarian then returned to the desk where he leaned against his chair.

Detective Petrov waited for the thickset man to depart before closing the door behind him and placing the file on the desk. He nodded towards the file, a sheaf of A4 papers enveloped in a green, plastic folder, and said, "There are inconsistencies in the witnesses' statements."

"What inconsistencies?" I asked. Using the chessboard metaphor, I felt as though my queen had moved into a prominent position.

However, Petrov offered me a blank look, suggesting that his game was poker and not chess. After a brief pause, during which he examined the file and its papers, he said, "Let us be generous and assume that Mikhail is innocent and that you are innocent; what is the motive for Ivan Simeonov's murder?"

"To keep the secret of the Mir massacre buried."

"You are convinced that the murder is linked to the past."

I nodded; it seemed the only logical explanation. To Petrov, I said, "As I'm discovering, the past, the present and the future are all intrinsically entwined."

Petrov fingered the file, turned a page and read. After absorbing its detail, he glanced at me and said, "You offered me information about a car; you said someone was following you."

I nodded. "From Hisarya, yes."

He ran a thick index finger down the page, pausing at the halfway mark. "The car belongs to Anton Yugov, a man of Russian descent, a petty criminal."

"Could he have murdered Ivan?" I asked, my tone alive with curiosity.

Petrov emitted a low grumble then shook his head. "Not his style."

"Then why did he follow me?"

The detective closed the file. He tapped its edge against the desk. "I will talk with Anton Yugov and ask him that question."

Another pause as another colleague entered the room. Again, a conversation in whispered Bulgarian then the colleague, a tall woman with dyed blonde hair made her exit, leaving yours truly and Detective Petrov alone, our nostrils twitching, responding to the lingering scent of her powerful perfume.

With his left hand, Petrov invited me to stand and, as I climbed to my feet, he said, "In light of Mikhail's confession, my superiors have made a decision. They have no wish to create a diplomatic incident and have your media swarming over our historic city claiming that we are holding beautiful British women in dirty Bulgarian gaols; it would damage our image and our tourist industry. So, for now, you are free to go. But don't leave the country," he added, his tone dark, suggesting that the Iron Curtain was about to fall.

"You're retaining my passport?" I asked.

Petrov nodded. His features moved the closest yet towards a smile. "You have already displayed that you have light toes so for now we will retain your passport, yes."

"And Mikhail?" I asked. "Is he free to go?"

In sadness, Petrov shook his head. "We will question him further. Maybe there is more to his confession than love."

Chapter Sixteen

Back at the mountain home, I managed a few hours sleep, showered then forced down a croissant and a cup of coffee before hitting the road, on my way to Mir. I was keen to talk with Maria Manova.

I arrived at Maria's house at 8.34 a.m. – a mine of local information, Petar had supplied the address. At Maria's, I sat in my car, released from the police compound, and observed as a young woman with large, heavy eyelids wandered from the house. Presumably, this was Valya, Maria's daughter. She staggered into a rusty sports car, driven by a scruffy youth, tripping over her high heels, offering the impression of a sleepwalker.

As the car sped away, I turned my attention to the house, a rectangular, whitewashed building, a bungalow with a low tiled roof, shutters on the windows and a satellite dish on a white, squat chimney. Maria's street was lined with many similar buildings, all bearing the stamp of a solitary mason, but all blessed with individual quirks.

At 8.54 a.m., Maria emerged from her house. She was dressed in a plain dark skirt, a short-sleeved blouse and a floral pinafore. In her right hand, she carried a large canvas shopping bag, which swung at her side as she walked towards her front gate.

After locking my car, I stepped on to the pavement, ready to intercept Maria Manova.

Deep in thought, Maria walked past me, her head bowed, her eyes staring at her flat, sensible shoes. She was so lost in thought that she jumped with surprise when I asked, "May I talk with you?"

"I am late for work." Automatically, she glanced at her wristwatch, which consisted of a large mannish dial on a wide leather strap. She glanced at the watch without really noting the time. "I should have been at Vesela Paskaleva's half an hour ago."

"Maybe we can walk and talk?" I suggested helpfully.

Maria paused. She sighed. "Very well. But we must walk fast."

We walked to the end of Maria's street, attracting the attentions of two nosy neighbours and a young woman pushing a child's stroller. A three-year-old girl sat in the stroller, blowing bubbles into the warm morning air.

As we turned the corner, into a wide street lined with high concrete walls, paved with crumbling tarmac, bordered with dry mud ditches, I said, "You told the police that I murdered Ivan Simeonov."

Maria's stride faltered then she walked on, her

pace quickening. "I did; I told them the truth."

"Yet you have no qualms about walking and talking with me, a murderer."

"Qualms?" She paused and frowned.

"Worries," I said.

Maria walked on, swinging her bag, swinging her hips. With her head held high, she stared straight ahead. "I am not a fool," she explained. "Even I know that a murderer who murders in secret will not suddenly murder in daylight, with witnesses around."

We had reached the local shops – a butcher's, a grocery store, a newsagent's – and true, people were milling around buying their morning wares, which consisted mainly of newspapers and tobacco.

"No, you are not a fool," I conceded. "What's more, you know that I did not murder Ivan Simeonov."

Maria paused as an elderly man doffed his cap and wished her a good day. Then, taking me aside, under the grocery store's awning, she said, "I saw you." Grinding her teeth and clenching her jaw, she added, "I saw you steal his medals."

I was inclined to challenge her statement, however, instead I said, "I believe that you're a good person, Maria."

"I am a good person," she said, her features pensive, her forehead etched with a frown.

"So why lie about the murder?"

Before Maria could respond, another shopper wished her 'good morning'. The jovial greetings reminded me that she was popular within her community, well-liked by the people of Mir.

Earnestly, I asked, "Who made you lie?"

Maria scurried on, past the shops, into a residential area. "I am late for work," she complained; "I must hurry."

"If you're in trouble," I called out, "I'd like to help."

She paused, dropped her shoulders then turned to face me. With a weary groan, she said, "I do not need your help."

I walked over to Maria Manova and glanced in her canvas bag. The bag contained a scarf, which partially concealed a handgun. I nudged the scarf to one side to reveal Ivan Simeonov's Soviet Makarov.

"Do you always carry a gun to work?" I asked, my tone laced with incredulity.

With a hurried hand gesture, Maria moved to cover the Makarov. "The gun fell into my bag and I forgot to remove it," she said somewhat lamely.

We were standing on a street corner, before a line of whitewashed houses. The houses were squat and pleasant, topped with terracotta roofs. The street was typical of many in Mir, with its roots set deep in the past, yet with satellite dishes and telephone wires buzzing in news of the present.

A rusty Moscovich trundled past, its exhaust billowing smoke. The smoke drifted towards us so we waved our hands in front of our faces, then cleared our throats.

Downcast, Maria stood on the street corner, her eyes fixed on her bag, on the handgun.

"If need be, you'd use that gun, wouldn't you," I said, stating a simple truth.

"To defend my family," she said firmly, "I would."

"That is the truth," I conceded. "But the gun falling into your bag is a lie, just as your statement about the murder is a lie." I raised my sunglasses and placed them on my forehead, then blinked as the sun stung my eyes. Although she stood in the shade, Maria blinked too, in nervous fashion, her right hand gripping, then releasing, her canvas bag, her upper teeth biting into her bottom lip. True, she'd dropped me into the mire, even so I felt sorry for Maria. With my voice even and friendly, I asked, "Who do you fear?"

"I fear no one," Maria replied stubbornly.

"Then why carry a gun?"

"I told you...," her face flushed, displaying her anger, "the gun fell into my bag, by accident."

I shook my head sadly then allowed my sunglasses to slip over my eyes. "You have many admirable qualities, Maria, but lying isn't one of them."

"Please," she begged, noting a gang of youths, who were eyeing us with suspicion, "people are staring."

"And people talk. Word will get back to the person who made you lie."

"I told the truth," Maria scowled, her shoulders shaking, her voice loud, carrying her indignation. "Nothing you say or do will make me change my mind."

From the corner of my eye, I noted that one of the teenagers was approaching, possibly to offer assistance, to shoo the stranger away. However, before he set foot on our pavement, I said to Maria, "At home, I'm an enquiry agent; people come to me with their problems; I help these people; together, we look for solutions. You know where I'm staying. Contact me; let me help you."

Chapter Seventeen

From Mir, I travelled into Plovdiv. Petar had supplied me with a location for Natasha Stefanova's beauty salon, a site to the north of the city, a few blocks short of the Maritza River.

I parked the Suzuki then stood on a street corner, to gain my bearings. Opposite me, I spied a computer store. The store contained four storeys with balconies and ornate railings decorating the upper three floors. Natasha's beauty salon was a smaller building, two storeys tall with large, plate-glass windows and a pink facade. A lofty, lean tree, one of several in the street, stood outside the building while, in the background, a green mound rose to meet the blue sky, its craggy features casting a shadow over the street, the Boulevard Sixth of September. The mound was an ancient fortress, Nebet Hill, while the street name referred to a day in 1885 when Eastern Rumelia and Bulgaria were unified.

To my right, on a street bench, an elderly man sat hunched, his elbows resting on his thighs, his thin lips sucking on a slim cigarette. He eyed me for a moment then offered a toothless grin. I smiled back then walked towards the beauty salon.

The fragrant smell of fruits, herbs and spices

greeted me as I entered the salon. Indeed, the fragrance was so strong that it made my mouth water. However, the beauty products lining the shelves informed me that I was in the right store, a temple to the feminine form.

A line of travel posters caught my eye, all highlighting Bulgaria through the seasons, all offering pleasant decoration, along with a photograph of three women in swimsuits. The women were smiling manically, the forced grins of beauty contestants. The winner, wearing a Miss Sofia sash, was indeed beautiful with long black hair and high cheekbones. However, the lady to her right caught my attention. Around eighteen at the time of the beauty contest, Natasha Stefanova was pushing thirty now, but still she retained her striking looks.

From her position, behind a counter, Natasha said something in Bulgarian and I shrugged, helplessly. She smiled, revealing a set of even, white teeth. Then she added, "You are a tourist? American, English?"

I nodded. "I'm on holiday, yes." Should I try to explain that I was actually Welsh, from that little country that bordered the might of England? I could hear my ancestors whispering in my ear, "go on, assert your birthright", while commonsense told me to let it go; I'd apologise to my ancestors when I got home; if I got home.

"How can I help you?" Natasha asked as she stepped forward to greet me. As with many Bulgarians of my generation, she spoke with excellent English, though she did roll her Rs. "A pedicure, perhaps, or a massage...we have a tanning salon at the rear of the store."

"You need a tanning salon in this climate?" I frowned while adjusting my shoulder bag.

"The winters can be harsh." She smiled, politely, her hands lively, realigning a range of beauty products, mainly lotions and face creams.

As Natasha busied herself, I took a moment to study her. She had shoulder-length hair, dyed blonde, with a natural kink. Her eyes were dark brown while her face was oval and blessed with wide, generous, brightly painted lips. Tall, at around five foot ten, she had a full, sensual figure, the sort of figure that was popular when Marilyn Monroe graced the stage. She wore bangles on her wrists, an assortment of beads and chains around her neck and long, dream catcher earrings in silver and onyx.

"You are Natasha Stefanova?" I asked, though I was certain of that fact: a poster in the window, captioned with Natasha's name offered a clue that even a bumbling shamus like me couldn't miss.

"Yes." Again, the dazzling smile and sparkling

eyes; if Natasha were a puppy, she'd be in all the advertisements.

Briefly, I returned her smile. Then I dropped all pretence and glared at her. "You don't recognise me, do you?"

"I'm sorry," she frowned, "have we met?"

"I'm the person who murdered Ivan Simeonov."

Her jaw dropped, to reveal a filling on a rear molar. Reminding me of a character from an Edwardian silent film, one of the ghosts from Charles Dickens' *A Christmas Carol*, she raised her right arm and pointed to the door. "I think you should leave my store," she stuttered, "before I call the police."

"And I think we should talk," I said harshly, "before I call the police."

Natasha turned and walked towards the window, where she busied herself with the window display. Her nimble fingers adjusted an advertisement for a cream that, apparently, gave your breasts 'that much needed extra lift'.

With her arms folded across her breasts, and while staring through the window, on to the street, Natasha said, "I have nothing to say to you. You are the murderer of Ivan Simeonov; I saw the murder with my own two eyes."

"Yet you fail to recognise me."

"I see so many people," she said, staring at the passersby, "faces become a blur."

"Even murderers' faces?"

Natasha turned. She brushed past me and walked into the store. At that point, a customer entered and I faded into the background. Taking her time, the customer bought a range of beauty products. I'm not saying that she needed the products but, put it this way, she would not have been out of place in an East German athletics team, c1984.

As the bell on the store door chimed and Helga strolled on to the street, I approached Natasha and said, "Were you with Maria Manova when you saw the murder?"

She scowled then, briefly, looked towards a telephone, which was resting on the counter. "I do not know Maria Manova."

"Where were you standing when you witnessed the murder?"

Her hand hovered over the telephone, her fingers shaking, her long elegant fingernails blending into a nervous red blur. "I have spoken with the police; I have no need to speak with you."

"Why didn't you intervene," I asked, "to try and save Ivan's life?"

Natasha placed a hand on the telephone. She stared at me through troubled eyes. She glanced at the phone, then into my eyes, and made a decision. She would not call her Samaritan, which suggested that she feared him or her even more than she feared me.

"Who made you lie, Natasha, and why?"

She bit her top lip and appeared close to tears.

"The person behind all this hasn't thought it through. They probably saw me as a soft target, a foreigner, an innocent abroad, a convenient scapegoat. But they don't know me or my background. I'm an investigator; I do this type of thing for a living; I search for answers, and I'm good at uncovering the truth."

"Go away," Natasha cried. She waved a hand in dismissive fashion. "I don't want to talk with you."

"If someone is troubling you," I persisted, "I'd like to help."

"Go away! Leave me alone! You can't help. No one can help."

I softened my tone and pleaded, "How can you be so sure?"

Natasha glanced towards the door as a young woman entered. They talked in Bulgarian then the customer disappeared into a backroom, possibly into the massage parlour or tanning salon.

"I must tend to my client," Natasha insisted. "But I will remind you, you are not at home now.

You should stop asking questions. You are in deep troubles. If you ask more questions, you will get into deeper troubles."

"What could be more troublesome than spending twenty years in a Bulgarian gaol?" I asked despairingly.

Natasha gave me a hard look, a look I considered alien to her. "These people are worse than our gaols," she insisted. "Believe me, you would rather go to gaol than meet them." The customer reappeared, poking her head through a beaded curtain. Natasha addressed her in Bulgarian then said to me. "Leave my store. Do not return. I must tend to my client."

Chapter Eighteen

Back at the mountain home, I discovered that the police were still questioning Mikhail about Ivan Simeonov's murder. Meanwhile, Alan had taken it upon himself to comfort Pavlina and Petar, and he was sitting with them in the living room. The conference was winding down so at least Pavlina could divest herself of that burden. Initially, Alan and I had considered hiring a camper van to wander, for a few days, through the mountains. However, my inquisitive nature and the hole I'd dropped into had put the kibosh on that plan.

While Alan talked with Petar and Pavlina about Mikhail and his predicament, I tried to connect with Faye.

I spoke into my phone, which was resting in the palm of my left hand. "How are you?" I asked.

Faye's image flickered into life and she replied, "I'm okay."

"How's Marlowe?"

Faye frowned. She pulled a face, wrinkling her dainty nose. "He brought in a dead mouse."

I nodded and smiled encouragingly. "He tends to do that when I'm away."

"I said I'd feed him," Faye complained, "but you never mentioned anything about dead mice."

"Pick them up by the tail and drop them in the pedal bin; that's what I do."

Faye shuddered. She grimaced, "Things like that give me nightmares."

"You're in a tough business, honey; believe me, there are more gruesome things out there than dead mice." I adjusted my position, rolling on to my stomach, on the bed. I propped my phone against a pillow, flicked my hair over my left shoulder and asked, "Did you deliver the bankruptcy notice?"

Faye hesitated. She glanced away from the camera and I could imagine her fingers, busy, tidying my already tidy desk. With a sigh she glanced back and muttered, "Er...almost."

"What do you mean, almost?"

"Well," she added defensively, "they've got a dog, a Rottweiler."

"The notice is for the owners, not the dog," I explained patiently; "you don't need the dog's signature."

"Yeah, I know." Faye placed her fingers on her ringlets. With her face displaying her agitation, she tugged at her ringlets and knotted her hair. "But what if he leaves his mark on me anyway?" she complained. "You might think it's fun, but I don't get my kicks out of Rottweiler's trying to bite my arse."

I tried to come across as a sergeant major, all

harsh and commanding. However, even to my ears, I sounded as firm as a soggy marshmallow. "You must deliver that notice, Faye."

"I will," she promised. Then, with a scowl scarring her face, "You doubt me, huh?"

"I don't doubt you," I said reasonably; "I'm just reacting to the evidence."

Faye sat back and gave me a grumpy pout. She thought for a moment, her fingers still toying with her ringlets, tugging at her blonde hair. Then, while leaning forward, she said brightly, "Tell you what; if, rather, when, I deliver the notice, you'll agree to take me on as your full-time assistant for a trial period, say three months?"

"Deliver the notice, Faye, then we'll discuss it."

"Oh, come on, Sam," she moaned, "give me a carrot; you should see the size of that dog's teeth."

I wriggled on the bed again, my nerve ends tingling, aware that I was making a momentous decision while my mind was preoccupied and addled.

"Okay," I conceded with a heavy sigh, "it's a deal, but at this rate, you won't have anyone to assist."

"Why," Faye frowned, "what's happened?"

I rolled off the bed and sat in a wicker chair. And from there I regaled Faye with my story. I told her about Ivan Simeonov, about his murder and the frame-up.

"Shit," Faye swore. "You're in the kak."

"Maria and Natasha are lying. The question is, why?"

In the corner of the screen, I could see Faye's hand, busy, with a pen and paper, making notes. For all her flaky ways and foibles, Faye had a good analytical mind, and she was loyal in a crisis.

"Someone's leaning on them," she suggested.

"Probably. But Maria and Natasha are not connected. They must be linked through a third party."

"The murderer?"

"My guess is, yes."

Faye tapped her pen against her bottom lip, with care, avoiding a small cold sore. Faye's life on the street had been tough and her system was still recovering. Therefore, occasionally, she suffered from complaints like cold sores.

"Hmm," she mused, "who'd want to murder an old man? I mean, what harm could he do?"

"People store up memories. Maybe Ivan knew something about the past that could disturb the present, and the future."

"Such as...?"

"The massacre at Mir."

In my mind's eye, I tried to picture the scene at Mir. A secret message had gone out, to the

Resistance fighters. One by one, they'd gathered in the forest to receive further orders. Then, machine guns in hand, the fascists had rolled up and mowed the men down. Some of the men had escaped, managed to flee the carnage, while others were captured, including Emil Angelov. Presumably, the initial message had been coded, or the men wouldn't have responded. So someone knew the code: someone aligned with the communists was in league with the fascists. It would take a heartless man to act with such duplicity, but such people exist, even to this day. The more I thought about it, the more I was convinced of Emil's innocence; I knew little about the man, except that he'd shared a special bond with his daughter; as a human being, he'd been all heart.

While I pondered the past, Faye made another note. She swayed out of the way and a meowing Marlowe came into view, his tail erect, his head dipping, inviting a caress. In absentminded fashion, Faye rubbed her pen against the cat's head then said, "Even if you're right and someone killed Ivan to bury the past, what hold do they have over Maria and Natasha? Why would they lie?"

"Fear?" I suggested.

Faye nodded in agreement. "That's a big hold."

"An indiscretion?" I ventured.

Now she grinned, displaying a wicked side to

her nature. "You think Maria and Natasha have been up to naughties?"

"Natasha, maybe," I conceded, "but Maria isn't the type."

Faye nibbled her pen while brushing Marlowe's tail away from the tip of her nose. After a thoughtful suck on the pen, she asked, "What are you going to do, Sam?"

"Follow Maria and Natasha; see if I can find a link to the third man, or woman."

"Watch your step," Faye cautioned.

I nodded at the phone. "I'll be careful."

"If I can do anything this end, contact me."

"Thanks, Faye. I will."

Before we could add another word, Marlowe's face filled the screen. No doubt, he could hear my voice, and the sound of my dulcet tones confused him. Leave the mice alone, sunshine, and I'll bring you a present from Bulgaria. Be a good boy and wish me luck, because I'm desperately in need.

Chapter Nineteen

I had a plan, to follow Maria Manova. Maybe she'd lead me to the third man, or provide a clue as to his identity. It wasn't a great plan, but short of donning a red cape and coming on like the Spanish Inquisition, it was the best I could think of.

The day dawned cloudy; a hint that August was drifting towards autumn. The weather was hot and humid, suggesting a thunderstorm. With bottles of water to hand and a packed lunch supplied by Irena containing banitsa – a cheese-filled pastry – yoghurt and fruit, I drove to Mir and parked the car.

I'd bought a new hat and a new pair of sunglasses. I'd also tied my hair back in an effort to disguise my appearance. Wearing a tee-shirt and shorts, I felt distinctly overdressed in this climate; that was one advantage of home – in the cold weather you could layer yourself with clothes and change your appearance. Here, you wore the basics, or walked around starkers.

At 8.49 a.m., Maria emerged from her house and strolled into a residential area. There, she entered a cottage with a bowed roof. The pattern repeated itself for the next eight hours: Maria walked, she performed her duties as a home help, she talked with friends and neighbours. Everyone seemed to welcome her; everyone returned her smile.

While Maria performed her duties, I studied the neighbourhood. I saw lots of people smoking and recalled a conversation I'd had with Petar. Apparently, Bulgaria is in the top three when it comes to cigarette consumption, along with Serbia and Greece; in Bulgaria, every other person smokes.

At one point, I glanced up to a telegraph pole to see two storks staring at me. They were definitely storks, but in my mind's eye I saw two vultures, ready to swoop.

In Mir, Bulgaria's communist past was still evident with small statues and monuments dedicated to former leaders. I recalled another conversation with Petar, about communism. I'd asked him about life during the communist era. He'd replied, "It was the best of times; it was the worst of times. Under the communists, you had security, full employment, a good standard of health care. Of course, there were restrictions, especially on foreign goods and on travel, but if you had the right connections, you could enjoy a good standard of living. In that regard, the East was no different to the West. The East applied controls and limitations, but in the West you're controlled too, through your media – only a handful of corporations own the main media outlets – wage restrictions and government propaganda. People in power serve their vested interests and the rest of us, the human ants, run around serving our glorified leaders. Only occasionally, do we stop and think, and when we do stop and think it usually leads to rebellion or war. But most of the time we are too busy running around, trying to control our own lives. That is the secret of government, be it a capitalist regime or a communist administration: you give the people just enough to hold on to, enough to lose should they rebel. If you reach that tipping point, you risk insurrection. Ask the younger generation and they prefer the freedoms of capitalism, freedoms that only money can buy. Ask the older generation and they prefer the security and certainty of communism. In the past and the present, you'll find people in distress while other people prosper; East or West, which is best? The Berlin Wall went tumbling down signalling the demise and failure of communism, yet the West is constantly in a state of austerity, which proves that unbridled capitalism does not work either. The answer: regardless of where you are, East or West, it's not what you know, it's who you know; connect with the 'right' people and you'll enjoy a pleasant life."

At the end of her working day, Maria called at

her local store where she bought thread for needlepoint, a TV guide and a romantic novel. Then she returned home. At no point did she glance over her shoulder, at no point did she become suspicious of me. Indeed, she walked around as though under a cloud, as though her thoughts were as grey as the Mir sky.

The rain and the thunderstorm held off allowing a gang of youths to gather in a park. There, they kicked a football around and drank beer from tin cans. A number of girls joined them, including Valya, Maria's daughter, though she soon disappeared from sight, dragging a teenager away by the hand.

Through the slats in the shutters, I could see Maria's television as it flickered. At ten o'clock, the lights in the house went out. I waited for another half hour then concluded that Maria had retired for the evening. Throughout the day, I'd seen nothing untoward, nothing suspicious. With my feet aching and my shoulders weary, I decided that it was time to return to the mountain home.

Chapter Twenty

Under a leaden sky, I set out after breakfast to follow Maria again. As with yesterday, Maria seemed preoccupied – I could have followed her on an elephant and she wouldn't have noticed. Also, as with yesterday, the pattern remained the same: a round of house calls followed by a quick visit to the shop then home.

At around six o'clock, I considered abandoning my surveillance for the day. Then Valya entered the street and wandered home. Five minutes later, she was back out on the street with yours truly in tow.

I followed Valya to the local park, where she met with the youths playing football. Another youth entered the park carrying a dozen cans of alcohol. The beer was passed around. Valya accepted a can, sat on a low wall and drank thirstily.

A knot of youths broke away, ran into the field and kicked their football around. Meanwhile, Valya sat talking with two of the young men, their body language suggesting that things were hotting up, about to become playful. After some kissing and cuddling and a period of intense groping, Valya took one of the youths by the hand. She led him out of the park, to a country lane. While adjusting my baseball cap and straightening my sunglasses, I followed.

Giggles and laughter mingled with birdsong as Valya led the youth into a recently reaped field strewn with bundles of hay. Arm in arm they walked over to a barn. After ascertaining that the coast was clear, they entered the building.

Meanwhile, I climbed over a five-bar gate and ran across the field, pausing at the barn door. The couple were kissing, reclining on the hay; he was trying to remove her tee-shirt while she had her hands in his hair.

Standing, Valya smiled at the youth. Then she leaned back, unbuttoned her jeans and unpeeled her tee-shirt. Partially naked, she held out a hand and the youth fumbled in his pocket for some Leva. Valya stuffed the currency into her jeans then pushed the youth on to the hay. I'd seen enough to establish a picture, to realise that she was prostituting herself, so I walked over to a hedge, where I squatted and waited.

With his hair dishevelled and his clothing askew, the youth emerged some fifteen minutes later. There was a spring in his step as he walked across the field, away from me, towards the park and his footballing mates.

Beside the hedge, I sat and waited. Then Valya wandered out of the barn. She made her way to the country lane where she sat on a low wall, making a phone call. With a smile on her face, she returned the phone to her jeans pocket. Then she leaned back, her hands resting on the wall, her heels kicking the brickwork in playful fashion.

Twelve minutes later a car turned into the lane; the rusty sports car, driven by the scruffy youth. Valya jumped off the wall into the sports car, which sped away.

I ran to my car, a jog of over a kilometre, realising that I had no chance of following them. Therefore, I reverted to Sam's Plan B: return to the known and await developments, which meant camping outside Maria's house until Valya returned.

So I sat in the Suzuki, thinking about this, that, and the other, gazing at the house, waiting for Valya, shivering a little as the day drifted towards evening.

Leaning towards the dashboard, I reached for my reading gizmo. The gizmo was a Christmas gift, from Alan. Over recent months, he'd been teaching me chess and I was turning into an addict. I'd even taken to studying grandmaster games, on my reader. That's because, whenever we played, Alan beat me, hands down. I was plotting my revenge, aware that it would take time, study and patience.

I was pondering why, in Moscow, in 1954, Mikhail Botvinnik had played 9. Be3 instead of the preparatory 9. h3 against Vasily Smyslov's King's Indian, when the rusty sports car appeared and Valya ran into the house. She reappeared, eighteen minutes later, wearing her glad rags – skin-tight leather trousers and a black, sequined top. The scruffy youth revved the car's engine, Valya jumped in and off they went. Prepared, and convinced that 9. h3 is all but essential, I followed them into Plovdiv.

In Plovdiv, Valya and the youth entered a nightclub. This meant more time for chess and reflection for yours truly. My bum was becoming numb when, at 2.19 a.m., Valya and the youth returned to the sports car. They drove into the darkness, towards a large public garden.

While the youth waited in the car, Valya entered the garden, named after the tsar, Simeon. Under the twinkling night lights, I observed as Valya talked with a young man. Square jawed and broad shouldered the man was wearing a long trench coat and a gold stud earring. Swift hands offered an exchange – money from Valya, a package from the man. At a guess, the package contained drugs, which Valya transferred to the youth in the sports car.

Valya climbed into the sports car. She accepted the youth's kiss, and fond embrace. The engine revved, the wheels spun and the sports car disappeared into the darkness. Meanwhile, I reflected that Valya was a part-time prostitute, at least, and probably a drug addict. No wonder Maria looked so glum. I decided to let them go and return to the mountain home. I'd discovered an important piece of the puzzle, though the full picture remained unclear. Therefore, tomorrow, I'd turn my attention to Natasha Stefanova.

Chapter Twenty-One

The sky was black as I drove into Plovdiv. Earlier, I'd managed four hours sleep, showered and breakfasted on croissants and coffee – despite the abundance of good food served up by Irena, my appetite was on the wane.

The plan today was to follow Natasha Stefanova, and phase one of that plan entailed camping outside her beauty salon.

I endured another bum-numbing hour sitting in the Suzuki, watching the women file in and out of the beauty salon. None of the women offered an air of suspicion or a nervous glance over their shoulders. At one point, a man entered the salon, which enlivened proceedings, then I nearly jumped through the car roof when a loud rumble of thunder roared overhead. The thunder and lightning were instantaneous, indicating that the storm was above us, and the rain came down in torrents, threatening to flood the street.

With my windscreen wipers battling the rain, I peered at the salon. I guess I was looking for something to tie Maria and Natasha together, maybe the man in the trench coat, the dealer who'd sold drugs to Valya.

After thirty minutes of intense meteorological

activity, the storm abated and the sun peeped through the clouds. After a further thirty minutes, it was as though the storm had never been – the streets were dry, it was baking hot and I felt overdressed in my baseball cap, sunglasses, shorts and sleeveless blouse.

I slipped my feet into my sandals and jumped out of the car. It was time to stretch my legs and offer life to the rest of my anatomy.

Using the shop windows as mirrors, I wandered the street, keeping an eye on the beauty salon. At lunchtime, Natasha emerged; with her head bowed, she skipped down the street towards a café, where she bought a toasted sandwich. After scoffing her sandwich and gulping her coffee – *indigestion ahoy!* – she returned to the salon.

At one point in the afternoon, the old man on the street bench smiled at me, flashing his gums. I smiled back and watched as he rolled a cigarette with one hand, displaying an art practised over many years.

An hour later a female road sweeper, middle-aged, dressed in green, took a passing interest in me as she pushed her broom in weary fashion. The streets of Plovdiv were generally clean, I noted, though blighted by the occasional sweet wrapper, cigarette butt or piece of chewing gum.

At the end of her working day, Natasha locked

and bolted her beauty salon then scurried through the streets. Pulling the peak of my cap over my brow, I followed.

Natasha was in a hurry; she paid little attention to the people around her, therefore she was easy to follow.

Our thirty-minute walk took us through the streets of Plovdiv, heading south. We skirted the old town by strolling along Tsar Ivan Shishman Street until we arrived at the East Gate of Philippopolis. Then we turned right at a church dedicated to St Paraskeva eventually arriving at a pedestrianized thoroughfare. The main streets of Plovdiv reminded me of home. True, the architecture was different – the elegant lines of Victorian Cardiff contrasted with the square solidity of communist-era Plovdiv – but the chain stores remained the same while many of the billboards carried advertisements in English.

We walked past a fountain, an attractive, circular feature with white foam splashing into a green pool, towards the Central Post Office and the archaeological dig. Next, we skirted a park, Tsar Simeon's Garden, the scene of Valya's drug exchange, before arriving at another square, squat municipal building, a public library. Maybe Natasha had borrowed books from the library and they were overdue, and that explained her indecent haste.

A mural depicting men – exclusively men – carrying swords and guns, documents and quills, books and parchment, covered the wall outside the library. Natasha's shadow fell over that wall as she walked up a flight of concrete steps, past a secluded area containing a red parasol, a small café.

While lurking in the shadows, under the shade of a large, bowed tree, I noticed that someone had sprayed 'trebor' on a wall. Walking past the graffiti, Natasha entered the library, a curious building with large, oblong windows partitioned with wide strips of concrete, forming an upside-down crucifix.

The library carried the name Ivan Vazov and was situated in a pleasant street paved with cobblestones and shaded with tall, elegant trees. I glanced up and down the street and saw no one suspicious so I decided to enter the library.

Libraries are my cathedrals and books are my gods, so I felt at home instantly, at peace. Amid the hush and reverence I located Natasha with ease – she was standing beside a row of books, an open hardback in her hand. Her eyes were staring at the book without really seeing.

Then a man wandered over to Natasha. In his mid-thirties and wearing an electric blue suit, he had short, dark hair, akin to a skullcap. His eyes were dark, bottomless and apparently vacant. Standing around six foot tall, he had a powerful, athletic frame and a square jaw set in a square unsympathetic face. His shoes were highly polished while gold glittered from his cufflinks. He looked like a muscular banker, and just as trustworthy. Was this the third man?

The man talked with Natasha in stern, clipped tones, offering a lecture. His words upset her and she appeared close to tears.

While Natasha fumbled with her library book, the man turned and walked out of the building. In leisurely fashion, I followed.

The third man walked into the city centre, pausing at a café. I noticed a vehicle parked on a street corner, a gold Opel Kadett, the car that had followed me from Hisarya. The third man leaned towards the car and talked with the driver. Then he tapped the car's roof and the Opel sped away.

The third man lingered at the café, sipping coffee, eyeing women, exuding an air of confidence and self-importance. In the private eye game it pays to stay one step ahead of the opposition so, from my position in the shadows, I gazed at the man and considered my next move.

The polish on his shoes, the lack of wear on his soles and his air of unbridled arrogance suggested that the third man walked only when he had to. He'd arrived on foot but, at a guess, would depart in a car. I'd lose sight of him if I went in search of my car, so I hailed a taxi in readiness.

As I climbed into the yellow taxi, the driver, a fifty-something gentleman with a balding head and full beard, raised an inquisitive eyebrow then uttered something in Bulgarian. I smiled helplessly and shrugged my shoulders. Then I pressed my palms down indicating that I wanted to rest for a while, to remain still. At first, the taxi driver frowned though, eventually, he understood my meaning and we sat in the car while the meter ticked.

Twenty-three minutes later, a busty brunette joined the third man and, laughing and joking, they walked to the street corner where they hailed a taxi of their own. Leaning forward I nudged my driver on the shoulder and said, "Follow that car."

In response, he merely frowned.

"The taxi," I tried to explain, "you follow..." I made another hand gesture, two fingers on my right hand walking after two fingers on my left. "Follow," I said, raising my voice, as though the decibel level would cut through the language barrier.

The taxi driver studied my frantic fingers. He gazed at me with a troubled expression, as though eyeing a madwoman. Then the penny, or I should say, the stotinka, dropped.

"Ah," he sighed, "sledvai tova taxi!" He raised

his left arm, slapped his thigh, laughed and we were on our way.

We followed the third man and his escort north, towards the Maritza River. There, they climbed out of their taxi and walked towards a swish apartment overlooking the river. I made a mental note of the location then indicated that we should drive on. Getting to grips with my sign language, the taxi driver duly obliged and we continued our journey, back to my car.

After paying and tipping the taxi driver, I climbed into the Suzuki. My feet ached and I felt tired to the point of exhaustion. Nevertheless, I promised myself that I'd return to the third man's apartment, at the break of dawn.

Chapter Twenty-Two

The following morning, I beat everyone to the shower. An hour later, I was strolling beside the Maritza River, watching the sun rise over the city.

Wearing a light grey suit with a fine pinstripe, the third man emerged from his apartment at 7.25 a.m. He climbed into a gleaming Porsche and drove into the city, parking his car in a street adjacent to Tsar Simeon's Garden. Unlike Maria and Natasha, the third man had his wits about him; he took a circuitous route along Ruski Boulevard, checking his rear-view mirror on a number of occasions. Consequently, I had to drive with circumspection and be on top of my game. Thankfully, Suzuki's are popular in Bulgaria and that fact helped me to blend into the background.

After walking to a children's playground within Tsar Simeon's Garden, the third man met with two bullet-headed men dressed in sharp suits. The men had a hard look and an air of criminality about them. Adjusting the lens on my camera, I snapped some pictures. I should have been capturing panoramic views of the mountains, not this potential parcel of rogues, but there you go.

The three men engaged in a brief, but pointed conversation, then the third man returned to his

Porsche. From the park, he drove west before turning north, heading for the Maritza River. Just short of the river, he parked the Porsche outside a large concrete office block, a block that looked so governmental and official its concrete should have been pinstriped.

In a side road to the south of the office block, I parked and waited, for the best part of two hours. Then the Fates rewarded me with a sight of the third man and his superior – a man bearing the trappings of political office: a briefcase, an expensive looking suit and a self-satisfied smile. Aged around sixty, the politician had a bald crown circled with a thick grey corona. His sideburns were bushy while his eyes were dark and hooded. He had a large mole on his right cheek, thick, rubbery lips and a comfortable paunch. He was short, standing an inch taller than yours truly at five foot six. He walked with an affable air, though even at a distance you could sense the sweat on his brow. From the shadows, I raised my camera and took some pictures.

The third man appeared to be the politician's secretary or minder and he escorted him to his ministerial car. Other officials and minders followed, along with a female assistant. Then the small convoy engaged gear and trundled down the road.

From the government building, we travelled east, into the city, to a hotel. Flags of many nations fluttered outside the hotel in a gentle, cooling breeze.

The security men stepped from their cars then the governmental party entered the hotel. Seemingly, this was a five star location and the minister was attending a business function. As I sat waiting, I wondered at the mindset of a politician. What did they crave – power, influence, wealth? And as for fame...was it worth the abuse, the hatred, the realisation that all political careers end in failure? What was it Bertolt Brecht said about the illiterate politician, 'he does not know the cost of life, the price of the bean, of the fish, of the flour, of the rent, of the shoes and of the medicine...he does not know that from his political ignorance is born the prostitute.' Politicians and prostitutes, natural bedfellows...no pun intended.

I sat in the Suzuki for two hours with pins and needles forming in my anatomy's widest part. Then, thankfully, the governmental party emerged and the small convoy trundled along the road again.

We travelled east to a small airport outside Plovdiv. The welcoming party offered smiles and handshakes then the third man and the politician disappeared into the foyer. From there, and two hours later, they returned to the government building.

What to make of my latest discovery? I needed local information. I needed to chat with Petar and Pavlina.

Chapter Twenty-Three

For dinner, Irena prepared surmi for the carnivores – cabbage leaves stuffed with minced veal, minced pork, spring onions, rice and paprika – and stuffed mushrooms along with baked cabbage for me. In light of my recent discoveries I found my appetite returning and I cleared my plate.

We were sitting in the living room, sipping wine, chatting aimlessly, when Petar's phone rang. He took the call, nodded several times, then relayed the message: "That was Detective Petrov on the phone; he says that Mikhail still admits to the murder, but his statement is riddled with inconsistencies. It is likely that the authorities will drop the murder charge and Mikhail might get away with a warning for wasting police time. However, for now, Detective Petrov must continue with the formalities."

Pavlina closed her eyes. Her hand shook a little, disturbing her wine. Nevertheless, she sighed with relief. Then, while opening her eyes, she turned to me, her face solemn. "So, once again," she said, "the police will look at you."

I nodded. With Mikhail off the hook and with Maria and Natasha sticking to their statements, I was the prime suspect, though to reassure Pavlina, and Alan, I offered a smile. "Give me a few more days and I'll be delighted if they look in my direction."

I offered details of my daily excursions, following Maria and Natasha. Also, I fished in my shoulder bag for the photographs, taken that day. A local store had developed the photographs, upholding their claim to a two-hour service. However, the owner had eyed me with some suspicion, no doubt curious as to why a long-haired British woman should be taking snapshots of local politicians and not the mountains and lakes. In former days, the authorities would have been knocking at the door with an arrest warrant. In that regard, Bulgaria had come a long way.

After I'd regaled my hosts with my story, Pavlina said, "You saw Valya purchase drugs?"

I nodded.

"You think she is a drug addict?"

I shrugged. "Sadly, yes."

"And someone is using the drugs as a hold," Petar interjected, "to make Maria lie."

"Either the person supplies Valya with drugs and is threatening to cut her supply, or he's looking to expose her as an addict."

Petar studied his wine glass in thoughtful fashion, running a finger around its rim. He took a sip of wine, licked his lips then said, "So, the man behind all this has drug connections."

"Maybe mafia," Pavlina said, placing a hand on her husband's arm.

Petar nodded. He drained his wine then reached for another bottle. "Russian mafia; the heavy brigade."

Pavlina offered her glass to Petar's bottle and he supplied her with a refill. She drank from her glass, jerkily, nervously, clearly disturbed by this latest revelation.

After refilling Alan's glass, Petar turned to me and asked, "And what of Natasha?"

"She met this man." I produced a photograph of the third man standing beside his Porsche. "Do you recognise him?"

In unison, Petar and Pavlina shook their heads. "No." Then Petar added, "Is he the pusher, the man supplying Valya with drugs?"

"I'm not sure," I admitted.

I produced another photograph, depicting the third man and the government minister. "What about him?" I asked.

"That's Nikolai Nikolov, a transport minister," Petar smiled. "He's a junior minister with plenty of local clout."

"What do you know about Nikolov?" I asked while nursing my wine.

"He is a local man, his family are from Mir. He

is a family man, wife and kids. He is a typical politician, you know, he will say anything, do anything to win votes, then will break his promises without compunction. He is always quick with an answer, with a reason or excuse. He has a genial personality and people like him for that."

"What about his broken promises?" I asked. "Doesn't he court resentment?"

Petar shrugged. He glanced at his wife and they exchanged a telepathic look, the look of a long-term married couple. He explained, "Just as in the West, people expect politicians to break promises; they expect them to lie. People know that politicians are compulsive liars. They have no expectations of them; they will vote for them because they like their personality; electing people for government is about presentation and image not about political truth or deeply held beliefs."

I nodded thoughtfully, sipped my wine and said, "And Nikolov is a local man, you say."

"His family are from Mir. Some of his relatives still live there."

Pavlina leaned forward, her posterior perched on the edge of her armchair. She tilted her head to the left then gave me a look tinged with anxiety and concern. "Nikolov is a man of power and influence, Samantha. If you ask questions about him, you must take care."

I glanced at Irena. Throughout our conversation, she'd been quiet, no doubt struggling with its twists and turns, with the pace of our language. She was rocking gently in her chair, her face set with determination, her eyes alive with a sense of destiny.

"I will ask questions and I will take care." I placed my wine glass on a small table and smiled at Irena. "Nikolov is a compulsive liar, is he? Well, it's time he abandoned his political doublespeak; it's time he told the truth."

Chapter Twenty-Four

A new day, but an old location. With the aid of a travel guide and a map, Plovdiv was becoming as familiar as the back of my hand.

I camped outside the government office block, waiting for Nikolai Nikolov to arrive for work. Suitably be-suited and with a briefcase in hand, he followed the third man into the austere concrete building, disappearing behind a glass door.

After a morning of bureaucracy and with the sun high in the sky, Nikolov emerged with the third man and a gaggle of attendants. They climbed into their limousines and drove through the streets of Plovdiv, east and then south, along Ruski Boulevard, to the Central Railway Station.

At the railway station, Nikolov found a television crew in attendance. Obviously, the minister was addressing a press conference, no doubt to reveal an important improvement to Plovdiv's rail network or rolling stock. With his minders looking on, their faces beaming with approval, Nikolov gave an assured, jovial performance, answering the interviewer's questions with a smile and an air of authority. The interviewer, a short, slim woman with dyed blonde hair, spoke earnestly, though her mounting frustration suggested that her hopes for a scoop or sensational revelation were founded on thin air. Nikolai Nikolov was a seasoned politician after all; he knew how to talk and yet say nothing.

From the railway station, the third man chauffeured Nikolov to a sports complex. After parking the car, they strolled into the complex, the third man carrying Nikolov's tennis kit and tennis rackets. While persisting in the role of invisible woman, the woman with no shadow, I made my slinky way to the rear of the complex where, through the wire mesh of a tall fence, I watched Nikolov play tennis with a younger opponent. Clearly, Nikolov was no Grigor Dimitrov, but he was surprisingly nimble for a big man and the laughter emanating from the tennis court suggested that he enjoyed the game.

Allowing time for a shower and general brush up, Nikolov strolled into the afternoon sunshine, climbed into his car and was chauffeured back to the ministry.

After three hours of mind numbing tedium – I could go into the detail, but I'll save you that agony – Nikolov emerged and climbed into his car. With only the third man in attendance, the car pulled away, out of the city, heading for the mountains.

So far, I'd been lucky – to tail anyone for any length of time usually requires a team, not an individual. However, as the traffic thinned and the road straightened it proved difficult to sustain my anonymity. At various times during the journey, I had to sit back and allow the ministerial car to go then guess at its destination.

In the distance, and with dusk falling, I noticed the car's tail lights as the limousine turned off the main road into the forest. Tracking the car through the forest alone, without being seen, was close to impossible. So I drove on to higher ground, unfurled my map and studied the terrain.

The map was highly detailed and revealed a number of holiday homes, dotted throughout the forest. Presumably, the third man had driven Nikolov to one of those homes.

I was pondering what to do next when the ministerial car materialized through the trees. With the third man driving, and alone, the car pulled on to the main road and sped towards Plovdiv. Was Nikolov in a holiday home, alone, or had he called on someone as a guest?

I decided to camp in a clearing, off the dirt track, and await developments.

At 10.14 p.m., a car cruised past. It was dark, visibility was poor, yet I swear that the driver was Natasha Stefanova. Natasha walked and drove as though in blinkers, so I decided to follow her.

As anticipated, the trail led to a holiday home, a

wooden-framed building, two storeys tall with a picket fence and a wide veranda. The picket fence and veranda reminded me of the Wild West yet, in general, the house had a Tudor feel to it, as though based on plans drawn up by Henry VIII.

While Natasha parked her car, a well-travelled Volvo, Nikolov strolled from the house to a small wooden gate. He stood beside the picket fence, his thigh resting against the gate. Then he opened the latch and greeted Natasha with a warm, passionate embrace.

From my position in the forest, sitting back, leaning against a tree, I pondered this discovery. Clearly, I'd stumbled on a love nest; Nikolov and Natasha were lovers. Where did that leave Nikolov's wife and children? What was the Bulgarian attitude to extramarital affairs? Such questions could wait, for I'd nearly completed the circle. The third man was linked to Natasha and so was Nikolai Nikolov. Without uttering a word, the minister had revealed the truth.

Chapter Twenty-Five

My surveillance had taught me that Natasha Stefanova experienced a customer lull around mid-morning. So, at 10.30 a.m. precisely, I opened her door and entered her salon.

"Can we talk?" I asked, dragging Natasha away from a shelf of hydrating masks, toners and cleansers.

Hurriedly, and none too convincingly, she glanced at her wristwatch. "I do not have the time."

"I think you should find the time," I suggested.

Natasha sighed. She glanced over my shoulder, to the window, no doubt hoping that a customer would enter the store. However, on this occasion, the Seventh Cavalry was conspicuous by its absence.

Nodding towards a shelf stocked with lip pumps, 'for thicker, fuller, plumper, bigger – *natural?* – luscious lips', Natasha said, "We must look normal, in case we are seen."

"What do you suggest?"

She thought for a moment then her beauty queen features brightened. "Why don't you step into the sauna?"

I scowled, a look lifted from the face of an Ugly Sister. "While you step outside the front door?" I shook my head in irritation and added, "I may look sweet and innocent, wet behind the ears, but I've a history of misadventures behind me."

Natasha stared at the floor, a floor patterned with mosaic-like tiles; it was a stare that signalled defeat. "What do you want to know?" she asked heavily.

I adjusted my shoulder bag, narrowed my eyes and said, "Let's start with what I do know. I know that you and Nikolai Nikolov are lovers."

Natasha's eyes widened, revealing streaks of red around the irises. "How did you find out?" she whispered. Then, before I could answer, "What do you want, money?"

I folded my arms across my chest and tapped my foot on the modern mosaic floor. "I want the truth. The only currency I'm interested in is the truth."

Natasha turned away, as though I'd struck her, as though the truth were a commodity edged with pain.

"The money for this salon," I continued, "it came from Nikolov's wallet?"

She nodded briefly then mumbled, "Yes."

"As a reward for your love?"

In a flare of Latin temperament, which suggested that Natasha descended from the Romans, she waved her arms around and said, "He asked me what I wanted. I said, I'd love to run a beauty salon..."

"And the man you met in the library, Nikolov's bodyguard?"

Natasha bit her lip. She shook her head and refused to answer.

"The bodyguard," I persisted.

"Please..."

"The bodyguard..."

She sobbed, on the brink of tears. Then she mumbled in a small voice, "Vladimir Kirov."

"Tell me about Kirov."

"No." Again, the violent hand gesture, though her voice lacked conviction.

"Tell me about Kirov."

"I hate you!" she screamed, then turned to walk through the beaded curtain.

I followed Natasha through the curtain, into the tanning salon. There, she leaned against a sunbed, her shoulders shaking, her back to me.

I allowed Natasha a moment to compose herself then said, "Tell me about Kirov and I will leave you in peace."

Natasha turned. She stared at me, her face streaked with tears. "Kirov is Russian mafia. You must not tangle with him."

"How did Nikolov become involved with Kirov?"

"I don't know." Natasha noted my scowl and added swiftly, "It is the truth, I don't know."

"What is Kirov's connection to your salon?"

She sat on the sunbed and placed her head in her hands.

"Kirov's connection," I prompted.

With nervous fingers, Natasha caressed her necklace, her string of beads. She tugged at the beads, her fingernails digging into her palms. She confessed, "Kirov uses the salon to launder money."

"Drug money?"

"I don't know." She looked up sharply. "I don't ask."

"And where does Ivan Simeonov fit into all this?"

"I don't know."

I nodded slowly then added without any irony, "You don't ask."

"Some things it is better not to know," Natasha mumbled, her head bowed, her hands resting in her lap, teardrops falling on to her fingers.

"But Kirov told you to lie over Ivan's murder."

She sniffed then brushed away a tear. "Yes."

"Did Kirov murder Ivan?"

"I don't know," she said quietly, "but my guess is, yes."

The bell in the beauty salon chimed to indicate that someone had stepped through the door.

Natasha looked up. She searched the walls, as though looking for a mirror. Then she walked over to a desk where she opened a drawer. From the drawer she removed a box of tissues and proceeded to wipe her face and dry her eyes.

While dropping the tissues into a wastepaper basket, she said, "You must stop these questions; you must drop your enquiry. Your inquisitiveness will get us killed."

"As things stand," I said, "Detective Petrov is poised to arrest me for Ivan's murder. I can't stop the questions or drop the enquiry."

Natasha made to push past me, but I reached out and grabbed her elbow.

"Of course," I said, "there's a simple solution to all this...You tell Detective Petrov that you're mistaken; you didn't see me murder Ivan Simeonov."

"And then I will die," she cried bitterly. "I cannot tell the truth. My life is a lie. I must go on living that lie."

Chapter Twenty-Six

From Natasha's beauty salon, I drove into Mir, to Maria's house. However, outside the house, I found a gaggle of neighbours, talking earnestly. I heard the neighbours mention Valya's name and the word *bolnitsa* – hospital. Clearly, something untoward had happened. So I jumped into my car and drove to the city hospital north of the Maritza River.

At the hospital, I parked by the main entrance and kept an eye on the main gate. It was odds-on that Valya had suffered a reaction to the drugs, possibly an overdose.

While the sick, the wounded and the visitors filed in and out of the hospital, I wondered about Valya, about the choices she'd made and the influences that had placed her in this predicament. Maria was a widow, so Valya lacked her father's guiding hand. Even so, the youth of today are advised and educated about drug misuse, are aware of the dangers, so what's the attraction? Maybe danger itself? Drugs were anathema to me, yet there were times when I courted danger, when the little devil inside my head insisted that I should wander close to the edge. A lack of parental guidance had shaped my personality, I was aware of that now, and my father's disappearance, walking out on me, at birth, had fashioned a rebel from day one.

At 1.53 p.m., Maria emerged from the hospital. She walked to the main gate as though in a trance. While standing beside my car, I called out to her then asked, "Are you all right?"

"My daughter..."

I nodded. "Drugs?"

"Yes. An overdose."

"How is she?" I asked.

Stoically, Maria stared into the middle distance. Understandably, she was too upset to talk.

"Here, come with me." I took hold of Maria's elbow and guided her towards a bench. There, we sat in the sunshine while children scampered over the grass, playing imaginary games, games of spacemen and aliens, of heroes and monsters.

We sat in silence for at least five minutes. Then Maria delved into her canvas bag, producing an apple. She offered the fruit to me and I took a bite. As I munched on the apple, I noted that her bag still contained Ivan Simeonov's Makarov, the gun nestling beneath a silk scarf.

While my mind worried about the gun, I said to Maria, "I know this is not a good time, but I'd like to ask you some questions."

She nodded. She'd removed an apple for herself, but it sat untouched in the palm of her hand.

"Valya is a drug addict," I said simply.

"Yes. She is addicted to heroin."

"Who supplies the drugs?"

Maria continued to stare into the middle distance. Although the children on the grass were screaming and shouting, laughing and yelling, making a hell of a noise, Maria gazed through them, as though unaware of their presence, as though her senses were numb, as though all feeling and purpose had disappeared from her life.

"Kirov," she said in a flat, dull voice. "Kirov supplies the drugs."

"And in return you spy for him."

Maria nodded. "Valya needs the drugs. She cannot live without them..."

Yet, she might die because of them. It seemed cruel to voice that thought so instead, I asked, "Where does the heroin come from?"

"Across the border...Afghanistan, Greece..."

"Kirov's men smuggle the heroin through customs."

She nodded, an automatic gesture, a reflex action. "Yes. And they use private airports and harbours."

"And this trafficking is assisted by Nikolai Nikolov."

Maria turned. She glared at me and for the first time that afternoon, I sensed a spark of life in her chestnut-coloured eyes. "He is a minister," she explained, "he has many connections..."

"Will you talk with Detective Petrov about this, tell him the truth?"

"I cannot." Maria stared into her lap, at her apple, at her fingers, her nails devoid of any varnish, at the red blotches, the eczema on the back of her hands. "If I speak out I will place my daughter in danger."

She is already in danger. But, again, it was too cruel to offer voice to that thought.

We paused as a ball rolled towards us. One of the children, a mischievous imp, eyed us with uncertainty, with a sense that adults were talking and something was amiss. I smiled at the boy, retrieved the ball and tossed it to him. He grinned, said, "Blagodaryuh (thank you)," then ran to rejoin his mates.

Maria dropped her apple into her bag, uneaten, while I tossed my core into a refuse bin. We sat with our own thoughts for a further minute then I asked, "Why did Kirov want you to spy on Ivan?"

"I don't know," Maria replied, her voice still flat and morose.

"You told Kirov that I'd been talking with Ivan about the war."

She nodded. "Yes."

"Why is Kirov interested in the war?"

"I don't know."

"Did Kirov murder Ivan?"

She turned, eyed me briefly then resumed her glum stare. "I am not sure, but I think yes."

"Ivan was in the Resistance."

She nodded. "He told you that himself."

"Were any of Nikolai Nikolov's relatives in the Resistance?"

Maria pursed her lips. She angled her head, as though thinking, as though fighting through Valya's predicament and the morass of upsetting and disturbing thoughts. "His father, I believe. Yes, Nikolov's father, Georgi, was in the Resistance."

This led us back to Hisarya and Emil Angelov. What role did Georgi Nikolov play in the Resistance? Was Ivan Simeonov a hero after all, deserving of his medals, or did he earn his honours and a comfortable lifestyle through suppressing the truth? My sleuthing instincts provided the answers, yet facts were needed to convince others, including Detective Petrov.

"I must return to the hospital," Maria said, offering an anxious glance over her shoulder. "And it is best if we are not seen together again."

I nodded. "I wish you well, Maria. I wish your daughter well. I hope she recovers."

Maria glanced up to the clear blue sky, its beauty and warmth offering a taunt to her thoughts, all dark and anxious. "God willing," she mumbled.

And, as Maria walked away, she left me with the thought that this was a woman who deserved God on her side.

Chapter Twenty-Seven

The Dimitrov household erupted with joy at 10 a.m. the following morning; the police had released Mikhail from custody, all charges dropped. He was a free man.

While Irena placed her hands together in delight and Pavlina embraced her son, Petar went in search of a wine bottle to celebrate. Patently, Petar believed in celebrations and he'd open a bottle of wine at the drop of a hat, yet the alcohol never seemed to affect him or alter his mood.

Petar hugged Mikhail then offered everyone a glass of wine. All and sundry accepted, though I declined; I had plenty of thinking to do and was in need of a clear head.

Mikhail quaffed his wine, laughed and spoke to his parents in Bulgarian. They joined in the laughter and although I had no hint as to the conversation, I smiled.

Then our faces became solemn as Mikhail glanced at me.

"I am grateful for your noble gesture," I said with all the sincerity I could muster.

"It was an act of love," Mikhail insisted, placing his empty wine glass to one side. "I would give twenty years of my life for you; I would die for you." He stared, pointedly, at Alan. "Would any other man say that?"

With his back straight and proud, Mikhail walked from the patio to his room.

After a pause, and some nervous chit-chat from Pavlina, to cover her embarrassment, we fell silent again; watching with unease as Detective Petrov and a female colleague entered the garden.

Petrov made a beeline for me, so I stepped forward to meet him. I said, "You're here to arrest me."

He offered a lugubrious shrug and a sad frown. "It is my job."

"What if we talk first?"

Petrov inclined his head then nodded. "I am listening; please explain; tell me your story."

"I know who murdered Ivan Simeonov."

He arched an eyebrow, instinctively. "Who?"

"Vladimir Kirov."

Petrov and his colleague exchanged glances then he said to me, "Explain."

"Kirov is Russian mafia. He traffics heroin, from Afghanistan, Greece. His poodle, Nikolai Nikolov, ensures that the borders are open and that the customs officials turn a blind eye."

"And what of Maria Manova's statement?"

"Valya, Maria's daughter, is a drug addict. Kirov is her supplier; if Maria didn't cooperate, he threatened to cut her supply."

"And Natasha Stefanova?"

"Natasha is Nikolai Nikolov's mistress. Kirov uses her beauty salon to launder drug money. The hold over her is obvious, and that is why she lied."

The female officer spoke rapidly in Bulgarian and Petrov nodded several times. With his expression thoughtful and with his left hand rubbing his chin, grazing its stubble, he said to me, "Maria Manova and Natasha Stefanova will corroborate your statement?"

"They are too frightened to talk."

Detective Petrov's shoulders drooped. He exuded a heavy sigh. "And so on your word alone I am to challenge a government minister?"

I nodded then offered a painful smile. "If you believe in truth and justice, yes."

"I believe in truth and justice," Detective Petrov said soberly. He added wearily, "I also believe in my pension."

"Then allow me to challenge him," I insisted.

Petrov shook his head, as though to clear it. He glanced at his colleague. She frowned then offered words of advice. After absorbing her comment, Petrov nodded quietly to himself.

We stood on the patio, the sun beating down, sweat forming on our brows, the tableau frozen. Mikhail had reappeared and was standing by a trellis, rich with clematis, his face serious, his muscles tense, his body coiled like a tight spring. His eyes met mine and I sensed that he was ready to challenge the detective.

However, with his face pensive and his brow burdened, the lines of strain showing, Petrov asserted himself and broke the spell. While frowning at me, he said, "Nikolai Nikolov will deny your words."

"Probably. But a skilled investigator can see the truth even through a denial."

Petrov nodded. Once more, he stroked his chin. I considered him a skilled investigator, someone who could sift the truth from the innuendo and lies. Furthermore, from his discussions with his female colleague I sensed that my revelations about Kirov did not come as a complete surprise; at a guess, Kirov was already on Detective Petrov's radar, a blip he was keen to extinguish.

"You neglect one thing," Petrov complained. "Why would Nikolai Nikolov risk his career to side with Vladimir Kirov?"

I turned to Irena and smiled. "I believe this lady holds the answer."

Irena stepped forward. With her fingers interlaced, resting against her midriff, she spoke quietly, yet firmly while Pavlina offered a translation.

"My father told me that he was not the traitor. He insisted that he was true to his comrades and the communist cause. Only Ivan Simeonov knew the truth, but out of fear, he refused to speak out. My father told me that I must never speak out, because to challenge the 'truth' would risk reprisals. But Ivan Simeonov knew the truth; he knew that Georgi Nikolov, Nikolai's father, was the traitor. Georgi spied for the fascists and betrayed the men of Mir. Georgi was responsible for the slaughter. Emil was innocent; he was a hero, not a traitor."

With tears in her eyes, Pavlina hugged her mother. And, as the women sobbed, releasing seventy years of hurt and grief, Alan turned to me and smiled. He put an arm around my shoulders and gave me a hug.

To Detective Petrov, I said, "If the truth leaked out, it would ruin Nikolai Nikolov's career."

He nodded. "So Nikolov sided with Kirov."

Petrov spoke with the female detective and she scurried to her car, to contact her colleagues. As she talked with her colleagues, Petrov loosened his tie and flicked a bead of sweat from his brow.

"Tell me," he said, his gaze and tone thoughtful, his leonine features displaying a new emotion, akin to anger, "how did Kirov uncover the truth about Georgi Nikolov?"

"Ask him that question."

Petrov pondered for a moment then nodded slowly. He was a man of the region, a man familiar with Mir's history. The truth about Emil Angelov and Georgi Nikolov had touched him as it would touch all the people of Mir.

"I will," he said, "I will question everybody. I will accompany you. And with Nikolai Nikolov first, we will talk."

Chapter Twenty-Eight

We travelled to the ministry in separate cars. The sun was high; the air was humid without a breath of wind. The flags hung limply on their poles; a haze shimmered in the distance while tar glistened on the roads.

As we parked our cars, Kirov and Nikolov emerged from the ministry, the usual entourage of minders, assistants and secretaries in tow. Even allowing for modern times, and the fact that government ministers are cosseted and cocooned like never before, it occurred to me that Nikolov was over-protected, for a junior minister. In all likelihood, Kirov supplied the additional muscle; the bullet-headed men in sharp suits and dark glasses were there to protect the mafia's interests rather than the minister's health.

While walking along the quiet side street, adjacent to the government building, Vasil Petrov flashed his detective's badge. The sun glinted off the silver badge and the bodyguards retreated, as though blinded by the display of authority, hypnotised by the badge's symbolism, allowing us access.

"Minister...Please forgive the intrusion. I am Detective Petrov of the Plovdiv Police. May I have a word?"

Nikolai Nikolov hesitated, his body arched, his heavy frame resting on the open car door. "Is this important?" he frowned.

"Very," Petrov insisted. "It concerns a murder."

"A murder?" Nikolov straightened. He stepped on to the pavement, closing the car door.

"The murder of Ivan Simeonov; the old man of Mir."

The minister raised a dismissive eyebrow. He puckered his rubbery lips then waved his secretary and an assistant on to the back seat of their limousine. "I read about that in the newspaper," he said wearily. "My department is transport; murder has nothing to do with me."

Detective Petrov slipped his identity badge into his trouser pocket, his hand easing past his holstered gun. He continued as though the minister hadn't spoken. "I believe you and your associate, Vladimir Kirov, knew Ivan Simeonov."

Nikolov's podgy fingers stretched towards the limousine and its shiny silver door handle. He gripped the handle and yanked the door open. Once again, he arched his body, to step inside the car. "I have never heard of the man," he insisted, his back turned to Detective Petrov.

"But you have heard of the massacre of Mir."

Seated now, Nikolov adjusted his clothing. He

nodded then gazed into the driver's mirror, to ensure that every strand of his thick corona was neatly in place and that the sweat was not too evident on his brow. "Of course," he mumbled, offering his reply as a casual aside.

"And you are aware that we have a problem with drugs seeping through our porous borders."

"The problem of drug smuggling is well under control," Nikolov insisted while glancing at his gold wristwatch. "Indeed, only last week we passed new legislation to crack down on the drug smugglers."

"But still the drugs seep through."

Nikolov sighed. He fingered his tie, straightened his jacket then removed a handkerchief from his trouser pocket. The handkerchief was white and monogrammed with two interlocking Ns. "Detective Petrov," the minister groaned, "this is not the time or place for a debate on drug control."

"I am aware of that, minister. But..."

Before Petrov could continue, Vladimir Kirov stepped forward. Without touching the detective, the minder ushered him to one side. "The minister is busy now." Kirov's gaze was fixed on Petrov, though his eyes were hidden behind dark sunglasses. "He has an important appointment; please arrange with his secretary to talk another time."

Kirov's sanctimonious smile indicated that the

interview was over. However, unseen and unsuspected, Maria Manova walked into the street, cradling Ivan Simeonov's gun.

The bodyguards, initially distracted by the conversation, reacted in an instant. While a secretary screamed, the bullet-headed men drew their guns. They would have shot Maria dead, but for Detective Petrov's intervention. Holding out his hands, he stepped forward and the bodyguards paused, their itchy fingers curled around the triggers of their guns.

"Vladimir Kirov, my daughter is dead," Maria announced in a dull, lifeless voice. "I have nothing to live for." With a trembling hand, she raised Ivan's gun. "Now you must die."

From the back seat of his limousine, Nikolov cringed and cried, "The woman is deranged; Detective Petrov, do your civic duty; arrest her; get her off the streets." With his white handkerchief shaking in his hand, Nikolov mopped the perspiration from his brow.

Meanwhile, Petrov drew his gun and we all stood in a tight circle; Maria's trembling hand raised towards Kirov; the bodyguards' guns trained on Maria; Petrov's gun vacillating, wandering from one person to the next, poised.

Then I had one of my crazy moments, a moment born of my upbringing and my tendency to act before employing deep thought. I stepped into the centre of the circle, between Maria and the bodyguards.

"Drop the gun, Maria," I pleaded; "if you fire, they will kill you."

She raised the weapon and took aim. "I have nothing to live for. I will kill them then I will die."

In reality, the bullets would hit her before she could squeeze the trigger. So I took a step closer and held out my hand. "No, Maria. Just tell Detective Petrov the truth; drop the gun; kill them with your words."

Maria hesitated; she glanced at me, at Petrov. Then she raised the gun again and, at Kirov, took careful aim.

"Please, Maria," I begged; "don't let them win; don't let them kill you."

The secretary was silent now; her screams had abated. From the corner of my eye, I could see Nikolov, trembling on the car seat. The bodyguards were poised, their arms raised, the silver burnish on their weapons glinting, while Petrov looked on with, apparently, ice in his veins.

Maria sobbed and shuddered. Her arm shook as tears ran down her cheeks. Her index finger curled around the trigger. It was now or never. With no room or time for thought, I ran towards Maria. I grabbed her wrist, her hand went limp and the gun bounced harmlessly at her feet. While Detective Petrov stooped, to secure the weapon, Maria placed her head on my shoulder. I wrapped my arms around her and she cried the rain.

Chapter Twenty-Nine

I was sitting in the small interview room in the Plovdiv police station, the airlock in the radiator assaulting my eardrums while the lingering odour of stale vomit turned my stomach; paradise, this was not.

The day had drifted into evening and I was tempted to place my head on the woodworm-riddled desk, to rest, when Detective Petrov entered, looking suitably grim.

"How's Maria?" I asked while glancing up.

Petrov leaned against the desk, a plastic cup containing coffee in his hand. He took a sip of coffee then said, "Her mind is overcome with grief."

"Will you charge her?"

Petrov shrugged. He swallowed the coffee then offered a grimace, pulling a long face. "That is for others to decide."

"And Nikolov and Kirov?"

He paused, his eyes thoughtful, his head bowed, the stubble on his chin picking at the collar of his shirt. After draining his coffee and tossing the empty cup into a wastepaper bin he said, "I believe your words; I believe that you are telling the truth and that Nikolai Nikolov and Vladimir Kirov are guilty. But without hard evidence I cannot act against a government minister."

I nodded then reached for my phone as it started to ring.

"Samantha Smith?" a dark Russian voice mumbled into the earpiece.

"Who's that?" I asked, my forehead creasing with suspicion.

"Vladimir Kirov. I would like to talk with you."

My frown deepened as I glanced at Petrov. He leaned closer while I asked Kirov, "How do you know my number?"

"I am a government employee...I know everything about you."

I nodded then said, "Talk, I'm listening."

"Minister Nikolov would like to meet you."

"When?"

"Now."

"Where?"

"The lake of singing fountains in Tsar Simeon's Garden."

"One moment." I pressed the mute button then turned to Petrov.

While scowling at me, the detective shook his head and whispered, "It is too dangerous; I do not trust Kirov."

"But we must act," I insisted. "We cannot remain passive. To free Maria, we must do something." I revived the phone and said to Kirov,

"I will meet you beside the lake in one hour."

Within that hour, Detective Petrov made the necessary arrangements to tail me. I drove to Tsar Simeon's Garden in my own car, the rented Suzuki. I parked the car, slipped into a light summer jacket and strolled along the tree-lined streets.

Adjacent to the park I paused beside a colourful children's merry-go-round, now eerily still and quiet. The brightly painted horses, cars and swans reminded me of nightmares from my childhood, of plastic dolls and woollen clowns coming to life, of spectral shapes patterned on my bedroom wall, ever changing as the moon filtered through the wind-tossed branches of an ancient tree. In those days, I had a one-armed, one-eyed teddy bear to comfort me. Now, I had Detective Petrov and his team for support.

I strolled through the park, passing the occasional night owl, the intermittent insomniac until I arrived at the beautiful lake with singing fountains. A large expanse of water with a sky blue lining, the lake contained a number of fountains, which were dancing rather than singing, rising and falling under the sympathetic shimmer of the night lights. Beside the lake, leaning nonchalantly against a park bench, stood Kirov. His two bullet-headed minders were in attendance, lurking in the shadows, one carrying an umbrella, which appeared somewhat incongruous and a trifle unsettling.

"Where's Nikolov?" I asked, my right hand brushing my hair from my eyes as a breeze cut across us.

"Not here," Kirov smiled. He was wearing his electric blue suit, highly polished shoes and a look of extreme confidence. He gestured, imperceptibly, towards the bodyguards and they inched forward. "Nikolov will meet you at a private location."

"We agreed here," I said, turning on my heel, walking towards the exit.

"The private location," Kirov insisted, grabbing my elbow and holding me fast. With his square chin, he gestured towards a bodyguard, the man carrying the umbrella. "You have no doubt heard of Georgi Markov?" he asked, offering a sly smile and a raised eyebrow.

I nodded. Indeed, I'd read about Markov. A literary man and a critic of Bulgaria's political élite, Markov had been poisoned with a pellet shot from an umbrella, in London, in September 1977. Markov's murder remained as a shameful scar on the face of Bulgaria's history, a despicable act that tarnished Bulgarians, wrongly, as barbarians in the eyes of westerners during the late twentieth century.

"The minister wishes to talk," Petrov said, his

firm grip guiding me towards the exit and a limousine with smoked-glass windows. "No harm will come to you."

With Kirov to my right, a bodyguard to my left and the man with the umbrella at my rear, I had no option but to comply and to hope that Petrov was still looking on, from the shadows.

While travelling in the limousine, sandwiched between the bodyguards on the back seat, I asked, "Does Nikolov know about the umbrella?"

In the front seat, beside the driver, Kirov turned, craned his neck and laughed. "Nikolov doesn't know what day of the week it is; he is easier to control than a puppet!"

We travelled out of the city, towards the mountains, which meant that Petrov would have to drop back, or reveal his hand. I knew from experience how difficult it was to tail someone along these dirt tracks with any degree of anonymity. Therefore, I had to concede that I was on my own, closing on Nikolov's love nest.

Inside the house, we found Nikolov sitting on a plum leather sofa patterned with brass studs. He was nursing a glass in his left hand, topped with ice and whisky. His white handkerchief poked out of his trouser pocket while a film of perspiration glistened on his forehead. Apparently, to the public, Nikolov was a genial person, a polished performer.

However, to my eyes, he was a frightened rabbit, trapped in Kirov's glare.

While the minders stood guard, flanking the main door, Kirov pushed me on to the sofa, beside Nikolov. Then the Russian walked over to a walnut cabinet where he removed a vodka bottle and a tall, thin glass. He splashed the vodka into the glass, studied the crystal with a well-practiced eye then consumed its contents. With a replenished glass in his hand, Kirov stood in front of an open fireplace, its logs stacked for the winter snow. He nodded towards Nikolov and, with the whisky glass shaking in his hand, the minister turned to face me.

"This is something I am forced to do," he mumbled; "you understand that."

"I understand that your father betrayed the men of Mir to the fascists and that you are complicit in drug smuggling and murder."

Nikolov glanced at Kirov, who merely frowned in return, his square, solid features set in uncompromising granite. After a nervous gulp of whisky, Nikolov reached for his handkerchief. He mopped his brow, lowered his head and muttered, "I have no hand in drug smuggling or murder."

I wasn't in a position to scoff, but I came close. I said, "Minister, that is a lie."

How did we wind up here? How did Nikolov wind up here? True, he had no control over his father and his father's actions but, as an adult, Nikolov had made some dubious decisions. Instead of admitting to his father's sin and sacrificing his political career, he'd sided with Kirov and so had condoned drug smuggling and murder. He'd taken a mistress, disrespecting his wife. While I was tempted to feel sorry for Nikolai Nikolov, I preferred to save that emotion for his victims.

"The sins of the father," I said. "When Georgi betrayed the men of Mir, did he stop to consider the burden he was bestowing, realise that the ghosts of a village would haunt you until the day you die."

Nikolov gulped his whisky. The ice rattled in his glass, jangling like Jacob Marley's chain. "We are not here to discuss the past," he insisted, "we are here to discuss the future; your future."

I nodded. "I'm listening."

"Ivan Simeonov..." Nikolov tried to smile, but it was the smile of an old man, a broken individual, "clearly there has been a misunderstanding. You are not implicated in the murder. The witnesses were mistaken. I will smooth things over. I will ensure that you are free to leave our country."

"Natasha Stefanova will withdraw her statement?"

Nikolov bowed, squeezing his flabby jowls against the hard collar of his shirt. "She will."

"And in return?"

"You will inform Detective Petrov that you are mistaken. You will clear me and Vladimir Kirov of all suspicion."

I paused to glance at Kirov. He was still standing beside the fireplace, his vodka glass on the mantelpiece, his hands behind his back, his jacket open to reveal a gun and a shoulder holster.

To Nikolov, I said, "I'm not sure that I have the power to meet your demands; Petrov has his own suspicions. Besides, I can't walk away from this as though nothing has happened; you are responsible for the deaths of Ivan Simeonov and Valya Manova and, doubtless, many other people who've crossed Kirov or become addicted to his heroin. From my time in Bulgaria, I have noticed many differences and many similarities; while I can't speak for the Bulgarian police as a whole I feel sure that I can speak for Detective Petrov; like me, he shares a thirst for justice."

"Then you take the matter out of my hands." Nikolov offered me a weary, sad frown then he turned to glance at Kirov.

While the minister stared at the ice melting in his glass, at his political career fading away, Kirov nodded towards the bodyguards and they stepped back, away from the main door.

Tentatively, I stood and walked towards the door. "I am free to leave?" I asked.

Kirov nodded. He walked past me and pulled the door ajar. Then he smiled, revealing a row of gold fillings on his lower back teeth. "Enjoy your freedom; enjoy every minute, every hour. Enjoy Bulgaria," he said, "for you will not leave the country alive."

Chapter Thirty

Detective Petrov found me, wandering in the darkness, along the dirt track. I climbed into his police car, debriefed him then he drove me home.

The following evening I was strolling along the hillside with Alan. We paused and he placed an arm around my shoulders. With my head resting on his shoulder, we gazed across the valley to the Rhodope Mountains, to the craggy boulders and the greenery, to the shadows and their hidden secrets, to the war memorial and its tale of tragedy.

In the forest, smoke spiralled into the air, the remains of a barbeque, while distant laughter and music drifted on the air, dragging my mind back to the karaoke and my pathetic attempt to sing. Whatever remained hidden within its history, the mountain stood at peace now. Forged through natural violence and turmoil, it offered a reminder that for everything and everybody peace beckons at the end.

"This is beautiful," I sighed. "This is how it should have been."

"Maybe next time," Alan smiled. He gave my shoulders a gentle squeeze.

I kissed him then said, "I complicate your life, don't I?"

Now, he sighed, a weary groan drawn up from the soles of his shoes. "Let's just say, the waters were less choppy before you arrived."

"Hurricane Samantha," I dug a playful elbow into his midriff, "the human storm."

He laughed then, with his tone sober and serious, he said, "You certainly stir things up, and usually leave the world a better place when things have settled down."

We walked along the hillside, along a dry dirt track that had been fashioned by animals, possibly goats. After climbing the hillside, we sat on the grass and watched the sun as it kissed the horizon infusing the sky with a bright orange glow.

"Nikolov wants to meet me again," I said, imparting information gleaned earlier that day.

"Uh-huh."

"I received a message. I think Kirov is behind the message."

"Uh-huh."

"It's a trap," I said bluntly.

Alan nodded. He took hold of my hand and gave my fingers a gentle squeeze. "A trap, which you will walk into."

"I have to; for Maria's sake, for her daughter's sake."

Once again, he nodded. "And for your own sake; for your own sense of right and wrong."

I turned and stared at Alan, brushing insects from my brow as they buzzed around me; blinking into the fading sunlight; trying to read his expression as shadows fell over his face.

"Does that make me a selfish or a bad person?"

Alan plucked a blade of grass from the hillside. He twirled it between his fingers, his gaze lost within the crags of the Rhodope Mountains, his thoughts first narrowing then brightening his eyes. "You're referring to the angst you constantly put me through."

I nodded.

He continued, "I had a firm line on you and your personality from day one. You're not a selfish or a bad person. I understand your motivations, what drives you, what's important to you. And, after all, a woman's gotta do what she's gotta do."

I gave Alan a grateful hug then said, "They're still leaning on Natasha, forcing her to stick to her statement. Even if she cracks at some point, this will drag on. I'll have to remain in Bulgaria, maybe under arrest, with you gone. We must bring this to a head."

"Uh-huh."

"I've made contact with Detective Petrov; I'll not walk in there alone."

Alan turned to face me. He placed a finger under my chin and drew my lips to his. "Walk out," he said between kisses, "that's all that matters to me."

"I love you," I said as he rolled on top of me.

By the time he'd rolled on to the grass, the sun had set on the Trakia Valley. In the darkness, his hand found mine, and our fingers entwined.

He leaned over and kissed me, turning the nectar into honey. He whispered, "I love you more."

Chapter Thirty-One

I was standing under the arch of the Roman gate in Plovdiv. Incongruously, modern scaffolding, either as a support or to aid repairs, surrounded the gate. The heat from the day had dissipated, cooling the cobbles on the streets. Night lights cast long shadows turning the innocent into the sinister, suggesting that angels were deadly phantoms.

My own shadow walked before me along a long, narrow street. I turned into an area of wasteland to find Vladimir Kirov leaning against an abandoned car. He offered me a smile, blew on his fingernails then polished them on his jacket. His jacket hung open, revealing the walnut stock of his handgun, which gleamed in the perfidious moonlight.

"Where's Nikolov?" I asked.

"Unfortunately," Kirov said without a hint of regret, "the minister was unavoidably detained."

While my eyes flicked from left to right, searching for shadows, probing for threats, I said, "So Nikolov has ducked out of our meeting. What a surprise."

Kirov straightened his jacket. He took a step towards me, his features hard and uncompromising, ghostly in the moonlight. "You have one last chance," he said. "Inform Detective Petrov that you are mistaken; admit that you have spoken nothing but lies."

From the left and the right, the bullet-headed men emerged from the shadows, their guns – Makarov's – weighing heavily in their hands. They raised their guns towards me and I stood there, my heart pounding, my breath shallow, perspiration seeping out of every pore. A little voice inside my head said, *"Run!"* But I stood there with fear gripping my body, with my senses heightened, with my nerve ends raw.

To Kirov, I said, "My mother brought me up never to swear, never to owe people money and never to tell lies. And, while I'm far from a paragon of virtue, I'd like to honour my mother and her memory."

"Then join her in her grave." With a grunt and a snarl, Kirov dived into his jacket and produced his handgun.

Then all hell broke loose. An arc light flashed on, blinding Kirov and his henchmen, while Detective Petrov yelled, "Police! Drop your guns!"

In no mood to surrender, the henchmen responded with rapid gunfire as they shot at the police and the police shot back. I was unarmed and vulnerable, so I dipped my head, released an ocean of adrenaline and ran.

I ran along the narrow cobbled streets with a location in mind, away from the gunfire, past colourful houses, their windows ablaze, illuminated by people reacting to the commotion, blinking sleep from their eyes, staggering from their beds in a daze.

I ran without effort, powered by the adrenaline, breaking Olympic record after Olympic record as fear compelled me into the night. Then I paused to catch my breath and take in my surroundings. I was standing in another narrow street beside a large metal disk, the cover of the town sewer or drain.

While hunched, resting with my hands on my haunches, I glanced up to see a shadow moving at the end of the lane. "Detective Petrov?" I called out. Then a bestial growl followed by the whine of bullets and ricochets as Kirov ran towards me, firing indiscriminately, without careful aim.

Kirov had lost all sense; he'd lost his composure. Whatever his motives at the start, and no matter what the cost, he was determined to take me down. This was personal – a fight to the finish. I had no illusions – it was him or me, it was do or die. Only one of us would step out of the old town alive.

I ran down another street, only to stumble as my toe caught the edge of a drain. Kirov fired and the bullet whizzed by, its trajectory disturbing my hair. The stumble had probably saved my life.

However, I had no time to reflect on that now; I ran for my life, towards the Ancient Theatre and its majestic remains.

"Where are you, bitch, where are you?" Kirov called out. The catch in his voice displayed his distress while his breathing, laboured and heavy, revealed that he was close by and desperate for air.

The sound of distant gunfire had faded and now sirens wailed, filling the night air. Presumably, hopefully, Petrov and his team had prevailed, had brought the henchmen to their knees, maybe to their graves. Petrov would instruct his people to search for Kirov; they'd head for the Ancient Theatre, our pre-arranged location, our point of refuge should disaster ensue. Using a fence as a springboard, I ran towards the theatre, my feet skipping over the large cobblestones, my toes barely touching the ground.

I was standing beside a gate, an entrance to the Ancient Theatre. The gate was locked with its bolt rusty, so I picked up a stone and smashed it apart. I ran into the theatre, down a bank of stone steps towards the stage.

Although exposed by the moon, trapped within its spotlight, the theatre and its columns offered a sanctuary, a target to run to, a place of escape. Surely, at some point, someone would respond to the commotion; surely, at some point, Detective Petrov would appear and bring the curtain down.

I ran towards a flight of six stone steps, skipped up the sizeable steps and scrambled on to the stage. A large archway to my left reminded me of Christians and lions, of people and animals tearing each other limb from limb. And the history books tell us that the Romans brought civilization. Yeah, well...if I should meet Caesar in the Afterlife I think I'd rather bury him than praise him.

Not wishing to see my innards spread over the stone and marble columns, I tiptoed through the ruin, seeking the shadows, my back to the wall. Then Kirov appeared on the stage, his jacket long discarded, his shirt soaked with sweat, his gun nestling in the palm of his right hand.

"It's over," I said to Kirov. "At any moment, Detective Petrov will be here to arrest you."

"If I kill you," Kirov said, "Nikolov will ensure that no one lays a hand on me."

He raised his Makarov, took aim and fired, and a bullet pinged off a stone column. I had no weapon; I couldn't fire back. However, I had my wits and a desire for self-preservation. I also knew that the Makarov carried an eight-round magazine and that Kirov had fired his last bullet.

I stepped forward, centre-stage, and Kirov raised his weapon. He squeezed the trigger, to no effect, to no sound but a gentle click. In anger and frustration, he threw the weapon at me. I ducked;

the gun missed; it disappeared into the darkness, bouncing on to the wooden boards at the foot of the stage.

"I'm gonna break your neck," Kirov growled. He stood in front of me, towering over me, his hands grabbing my shoulders, moving towards my throat. Inside my head, the lights dimmed, as house lights dim when they experience a brief power cut. With my senses returning, I brought my knee up and connected with Kirov's groin. He uttered an oath, in raucous Russian, then doubled up in pain.

After years of domestic abuse, and receiving threats at the dawn of my detective agency, I'd decided to enrol in a self-defence course. That course taught me to look for vulnerable targets, such as the eyes, the solar plexus, the fingers and the groin; to counterattack as soon as possible; to strike once and step back; to place meaning into every action and not become involved in a power struggle or grappling match.

I put that training to good effect, striking at Kirov's groin, at his knees, at his face, using my quick feet and slim body to my advantage, combating his power and aggression with my agility and nimble frame.

However, there were times when Kirov breached my defences – struck me forcibly, grabbed my arm or bruised my skin. Our brawl was not pretty; in fact, it was damned ugly, a blight on my femininity, an act of sin.

After blow and counterblow, I held a slight advantage on account of my agility and my superior physical fitness. The run through the old streets had been draining, despite all the adrenaline. Also, Kirov's bloodshot eyes and barbarian demeanour revealed that the drugs he peddled were no stranger to him. A man of his physique should have claimed the advantage; however, heroin can reduce the strongest Hercules to the weakest Achilles, turn a man of iron into a rope of sand.

Above us, the Roman statues looked down, along with the spirits of past players, the ghosts of two thousand years. Those actors had graced the stage while we threatened to desecrate it. *Ah well, Samantha, no time for cultural niceties now.* I brought my leg up, flexed my knee and kicked Kirov repeatedly in the groin.

"That's for Maria!" I screamed, barely holding on to the threads that I called sanity.

Another man would have rolled around in agony. However, Kirov was made of sterner stuff. Although he was suffering, physically, he still offered a potent threat, which he demonstrated while making a powerful lunge.

I stepped to one side, avoided his lunge, then watched in horror as he drew a knife from a scabbard, attached to his right calf. The knife came as a surprise, an unpleasant surprise, and I was left to reflect that, maybe, I'd underestimated my opponent. Although doubled up in pain, Kirov moved towards me, his right hand high, the long, jagged blade glinting in the moonlight.

He was about to thrust the knife when a gunshot echoed in the theatre. I turned, to stare into the darkness, to see Detective Petrov poised, crouched, his weapon couched in two hands.

Petrov's aim had been true; his bullet had entered Kirov's body, bringing the murderer to his knees, to his side then finally to the wooden boards as he rolled and fell off the stage.

With his colleagues around him, Petrov walked forward, to examine the body. Kirov was dead, Nikolov discredited; we had won. Yet the victory seemed hollow – no action could restore Ivan and Valya to life and health while only time could ease Maria's pain. And how much time? How long is a length of rope?

Petrov offered a helping hand and I stepped down from the stage. Instinctively I knew that Kirov wouldn't be alone in shaking hands with the Devil; that the gunfight at the waste ground had proved decisive – that his two henchmen would flank him as they wandered through Hell.

Petrov's solicitous gaze carried with it a

considerate question. I nodded, answering in the affirmative; I was battered and bruised, mentally and physically exhausted, but I was all right.

The detective placed his gun in its holster. He offered a guiding hand and together we walked away from the stage. With our sights set on the night lights of Plovdiv, we strolled out of the theatre into the future away from the past, yet aware that this moment would live with us forever, in the realisation that after a violent act nothing stays the same.

Chapter Thirty-Two

Back at the police station in Plovdiv, I offered my statement, sipped tar masquerading as coffee and contemplated crawling into bed. However, before I could rest, Detective Petrov wanted a word, or two.

We were sitting at the woodworm infested table; yours truly parked on a straight-backed chair while Petrov reversed a similar chair and leaned into it. He ran a hand through his hair, sighed and said, "It is not every day that I shoot a man."

I nodded, paused then asked, "How do you feel?"

"Uncomfortable."

Again, I nodded. I thought back to an incident involving an obnoxious, perverted woman and a fatal shooting at an abandoned quarry. "Even when you fire in self-defence," I said, "it disturbs you; I shot a woman to save my own life, yet she still crowds my nightmares."

Petrov leaned towards the table, pressing his weight against the back of the chair. He studied my face, my arms, my neck, running a solicitous eye over the cuts and bruises, which were plentiful, courtesy of Kirov.

"He hurt you," Petrov said. "How do you feel?"

I shrugged. "I bruise easily, I heal quickly; put it down to years of experience."

Petrov pursed his lips. He gave me an old-fashioned look, the sort of look tendered by heroes in old black-and-white movies. "Maybe I should strike a medal for you," he said, "for your bravery when confronting Maria, for your courage when challenging Kirov."

I smiled at the thought then dismissed it as fanciful. "I don't believe in medals. Besides, what was it Mark Twain said...'It's not the size of the dog in the fight, it's the size of the fight in the dog.' I'm a mongrel, Detective Petrov, a scrapper, and I know it. Anyway, I'm not brave; I just follow my instincts, wherever they lead."

With the old-fashioned look still fixed on his face, Detective Petrov opened a file and placed it on the desk. From the file, he removed a document. "Your passport. We have your statement. You are free to leave."

I accepted my passport from Petrov's large, hirsute hand and placed it in my shoulder bag. While I tidied the items in my bag – as usual, it was cluttered – I thought of Maria and asked about her welfare. "I hope Maria is well. Even though she made some bad decisions, she tried to protect her daughter."

"I have spoken with her about Kirov and the

shooting at the theatre. She is grateful and more lucid; I think she is regaining her mind."

"Will she stand trial?"

Petrov shrugged a weary shoulder. "That is for others to decide. But even at a trial, when the facts are known, when the people hear that a grieving mother tried to shoot a drug-running Mafioso...would you pronounce a sentence of guilty?"

"I would not," I said, then asked, "Have you talked with Natasha Stefanova?"

"She is still reticent; even with Kirov dead she is reluctant to change her story. With Natasha, fear holds her tongue."

"As it did with Ivan, for all those years."

Petrov closed the file. He pushed the documents to his left then tapped his breast pocket as though searching for cigarettes, a ritual he'd performed on a previous occasion. The rueful expression on his face offered a reminder, to himself and the onlooker, that he'd kicked the habit some time ago.

"Natasha's words will prove an irrelevance," Petrov said. "Nikolai Nikolov is trying to salvage his reputation. He is talking of threats made against him, of blackmail. Like a true politician he is blending the truth with lies and half-lies, but instead of tying the populace in ribbons, he is binding himself in knots."

"Nikolov will have to resign."

Petrov nodded. "At the very least."

He stood, then with his right hand, he led me towards the door.

As we strolled along the corridor, towards the exit, Petrov said, "This is not the end, it is a fresh beginning. Kirov is dead, but another will take his place. The network will rebuild and again they will smuggle drugs across the border to kill daughters like Valya." He placed a hand to the back of his neck and stretched his aching muscles. "The war is never-ending."

I nodded then said, "But still we fight in the hope that small battles can be won."

Petrov opened the main door and we walked to my car.

In the car park, I asked, "How did Kirov uncover the truth about the Mir massacre?"

Petrov glanced over his shoulder, as though to ensure that no one was listening. The day had dawned, offering unbroken sunshine. The temperature would touch forty degrees Celsius by noon and those with the opportunity would sleep. Today, I would count myself among their number.

"The Mir massacre...agents, double-agents, the murky world of spies," Petrov said. "An official in the Kremlin uncovered a document and sold it to the mafia. The mafia then sent Kirov along to lean on Nikolov; at least, that is Nikolov's version of the truth."

"A secret so old, yet it retains such a hold."

Petrov nodded. "The people of Mir are country people; they have long memories. The sins of Georgi Nikolov became the sins of his son, Nikolai. If the people had known the truth, Nikolai would not have won one vote, let alone enjoyed a political career."

At the car, I opened the driver's door and threw my shoulder bag on to the passenger seat. I held out my hand and offered it to Detective Petrov. "Thank you," I said. "Thank you for your help, thank you for everything."

"My pleasure." Petrov offered a slight bow, bending at the waist. Instead of shaking my hand, he leaned forward to kiss it. "But the next time you visit our country," he said while straightening, "please try a holiday resort. I can recommend the beaches at Varna; they are very nice."

I nodded and smiled. As I placed the Suzuki into gear, I noticed that Detective Petrov was still looking doleful and morose. How to cheer him up? Then I recalled a joke, supplied by my old friend, Detective Inspector 'Sweets' MacArthur.

"Clearly, the Romans left their mark on your fascinating city, so maybe you're familiar with this

Latin motto...Volvo, Video, Velcro...I came, I saw, I stuck around..."

As the Suzuki trundled down the road, away from the Plovdiv police station, I glanced in my rear-view mirror, at Detective Petrov. I couldn't be sure, but maybe that was a smile playing around his lips. Or maybe it was wind.

Chapter Thirty-Three

We'd packed our suitcases and enjoyed a stroll through the valley. Now I was sitting in a wicker chair, my feet resting on the bed, my fingers busy with my phone as I tried to connect with Faye.

"Hi, Sam," Faye said brightly, her video image sparking into life. Faye's hair was neatly combed, her face stylishly made-up while her sunny disposition revealed that she was pleased with herself. However, before moving on to the reason for that pleasure I told her about my dealings with Nikolov and Kirov.

"So, you're off the hook," Faye sighed with relief.

I nodded at the phone. "Home soon. But what about you; did you deliver the bankruptcy notice?"

Faye gave me a coy look; all shy and coquettish, then she switched her smile on to full beam. "All delivered and signed for."

"What about the dog?" I asked.

"I waited for the owner to take him out for a walk then got the wife to sign."

"See," I raised a hand and waved it in acknowledgement, "the solution is often a simple one, if you take the time to look."

Faye continued to grin at me, her pleasure

palpable, her expression suggesting that she was the cat who'd scoffed the cream.

"So, what about it, Sam?" she asked, a frown now creasing her forehead, indicating that her question was serious.

"What about what?"

"Will you take me on, full-time; a trial period, three months."

I bit my lower lip and lapsed into deep thought. True, a clutch of prestigious cases had raised my profile recently and my workload was steady, if not spectacular; I was in need of an assistant, part-time. Could I stretch that into a full-time position? With a bit of financial juggling, maybe, though money would be tight.

I was still high on adrenaline, floating down from recent events, recovering from my ordeal. Consequently, I spoke from the heart, not from my business head.

"The pay will be basic..."

"I'm not after the money," Faye moaned, "a chance, that's all I want."

I nodded. She'd been through a lot in her young life; she deserved that chance. "I'll take you on," I said.

"Fracking hell!" Faye glared at the phone. She screamed like a banshee released from its chains. "Fracking hell!" she repeated and screamed again.

In the corner of the screen, I could see Marlowe, or rather his tail. Faye's excitement had upset him, had disturbed his sleep, and now he was heading for the window, for the delights of the alley, no doubt to chase mice, to pursue his carnal ambitions, to boss the neighbourhood.

"Thanks, Sam," Faye said, her excitement still evident, her smile still radiant, though she'd regained her composure. "See you soon!"

I closed the phone then strolled on to the patio to join Alan and our hosts.

Pavlina greeted me with a warm smile. Indeed, after a fraught fortnight, she seemed tranquil, at ease.

I returned her smile and said, "Thank you for your hospitality. You have a beautiful home."

"Thank you," Pavlina replied. "It has been an emotional journey but, finally, my mother can share the truth about Emil; instead of hiding his name in disgrace, we can celebrate Emil as a hero."

We embraced, kissed each other on the cheeks and vowed to keep in touch.

"The conference was a great success," Alan said, stepping forward to thank Pavlina. "You must organise another one."

In reply, Pavlina nodded and smiled.

Then with a knowing grin illuminating his face, Petar advanced and presented Alan with a bottle of wine, which my paramour duly accepted. "From my vineyard," Petar announced while tapping his nose in conspiratorial fashion, as though imparting a great secret. "A favourite vintage; save it for a special occasion."

Alan nodded. He cradled the wine as a father might cradle a baby. "Thanks, Petar. And nice meeting you again."

The conviviality was thicker than the insects, which danced and buzzed over the water, swooping and humming above the small swimming pool. However, the laugher soon stopped and we all fell silent as Mikhail wandered on to the patio.

"I will wait for your return," he said to me, his tone sombre and serious. "No matter how many days, how many nights, I will wait for you."

"Oh, Mikhail..." He wasn't in love with me; I could have been anyone; he was in love with the idea of being in love. Nevertheless, his words and gestures had touched me deeply, so I gave him a big, affectionate hug.

We were loading the suitcases into Petar's car when Irena appeared on the patio. She grinned at me then suggested that we should go for a drive.

As Irena mimicked the action of steering a car, I asked Alan, "We have time?"

He glanced at his wristwatch then nodded. "A little."

I turned to Irena and we both smiled. As a thank you, I stood on tiptoe and kissed Alan on the lips. "You go ahead. I'll meet you at the airport; I'll catch you up."

Irena gathered flowers from her garden, a colourful, fragrant bouquet of poppies, lilies, lavender and roses. Then we drove to Hisarya to the stone ruin, the hermit's cell that Emil had once called home.

With reverence, Irena placed the flowers beside a spring. She whispered a short prayer, which mentioned my name, Samantha.

As we stood on the grassy mound, gazing at the spring, I said, "Your father was a hero." I tapped my left breast, as though caressing a line of medals.

"Da," Irena grinned and wobbled her head.

"But you knew that anyway. Emil was your father; he was a hero to you in every sense."

"Da." Irena offered an even broader grin, which touched her eyes and made them sparkle.

"But now everyone will know the truth about the Hermit of Hisarya."

Irena leaned forward. She hugged me and said in English, "I will die happy."

Maybe, I thought, my head resting on Irena's shoulder, my eyes gazing at the spring, at the sparkling, clear water, at the bouquet of flowers, presented with eternal love. Maybe, Irena, but not yet, for before that fateful day, you have plenty of roses to tend first.

SAM'S SONG

by Hannah Howe

Love Hurts. For Derwena de Caro, songstress, female icon, teenage dream, success brought drugs, alcohol and a philandering boyfriend. It also brought wealth, fame and a stalker, or so she claimed. And that's where I came in, to investigate the identity of the stalker, little realising that the trail would lead to murder and a scandal that would make the newspaper headlines for months on end.

Love Hurts. For me, Samantha Smith, Enquiry Agent, love arrived at the end of a fist. First, I had to contend with an alcoholic mother, who took her frustrations out on me throughout my childhood, then my husband, Dan, who regarded domestic violence as an integral part of marriage. But I survived. I obtained a divorce, kept my sense of humour and retained an air of optimism. I established my business and gained the respect of my peers. However, I was not prepared for Dan when he re-entered my life, or for the affection showered on me by Dr Alan Storey, a compassionate and rather handsome psychologist.

Sam's Song. This is the story of a week that changed my life forever.

LOVE AND BULLETS

by Hannah Howe

It had been a week since the incident at the abandoned quarry, a week since I'd shot and killed someone, a week since my ex-husband had been murdered. It had been an emotional week. But life goes on. I'd been hired to discover who was sending death threats to Dr Ruth Carey, a controversial psychiatrist. The trail led to two high-powered villains and soon the death threats were aimed at me, threats that increased following two murders.

Meanwhile, after years of domestic violence, I was trying to make sense of my private life. Dr Alan Storey, a prominent psychologist, claimed that he loved me, and I was strongly attracted to him. But the years of domestic abuse had scarred me emotionally and I was reluctant to commit to a relationship.

Love and Bullets is the story of a dramatic week in my life, a week of soul-searching, self-discovery and redemption.

THE BIG CHILL

by Hannah Howe

"Emergency!" "Christ! Who shot her?" "Don't know." "What a mess." "Better call Dr Warburton."

Bright lights. A sharp, antiseptic smell. Pain. Nausea. Feel so weak. The cat, who'll feed the cat? "Marlowe." "She's babbling." "She's lost a lot of blood." *Blackness.* "Have we lost her?" *I don't want to die!*

A jumble of images, my mother, my father, but his face is so vague. "Daddy!" *Nothing.* A man scowling, with a needle. "I'm going to put you to sleep. You won't feel a thing. Just count backwards from ten..." "Ten, nine, eight..."

Aching all over. Can't move my shoulder or my arm. Very tired. More nightmares; too black to dwell on; make them go away...

Sweating. Drowning. I catch my breath, like breathing for the first time. Eyes blink awake. Gasping. Try to rise, but head hurts too much. I ache all over, but I'm alive!

I was alive. But with a snowstorm gripping the city and with an unknown assassin closing in, I faced the most dangerous moment of my life and the very real prospect of feeling the big chill.

RIPPER

by Hannah Howe

"I love breaking the rules." – Cardiff Jack

Someone was murdering prostitutes, placing their bodies in the Bay and covering them with roses. To the media, he was 'Cardiff Jack', to the rest of us he was a man to avoid and fear.

Meanwhile, I was searching for Faye Collister, a prostitute. Why was Faye, a beautiful woman from a privileged background, walking the streets? Why had she disappeared? And what was her connection to Cardiff Jack?

As questions tumbled into answers, I made a shocking discovery, a discovery that would resonate with me for the rest of my life.

Ripper – the story of a week in my life that reshaped the past, disturbed the present and brought the promise of an uncertain future.

Web Links

For details about Hannah Howe and her books, please visit http://hannah-howe.com

For more details about Sam the Private Eye, please visit http://sam-private-eye.com

To listen to audio book samples from the Sam Smith Mystery Series please visit
https://www.youtube.com/user/goylake